ISBN 978-1-0689591-0-3
A Fistful of Lollies
Copyright Cheryl Suzanne Rosbak 2024
All rights reserved
This is a work of fiction
Cover by Cheryl Rosbak
Absolutely no generative AI (LLMs) were used in the production of this book.

1

Josie and Simon would argue about that day in first grade for the rest of their lives together.

Details they agreed on:
It was Halloween
Simon's candy went missing

Details in dispute:
Josie stole Simon's candy

Even at the time Josie claimed innocence: it wasn't stealing if the candy was sitting beside the bowl the teacher set out for anyone to take from. And she didn't profit from it; she gave it to her twin sister, Bianca, who had dropped all hers in the snow. That's what you were supposed to do at Halloween, give candy to people. How was she to know it belonged to the new kid? And anyway, he'd called her a peepee head, which was way worse.

Several lectures from teachers and parents and two forced apologies later, everyone thought the matter was settled.

It wasn't, and wouldn't be for another twenty-five years.

"Bianca! Where's that praline?"

"Cooling!" Josie could barely hear her sister over the whump of the heating coming on for the first time that fall. The temperature had dropped far and fast the previous day, and Josie couldn't put off turning on the furnace in the building any longer or her candies—and her tenants—would suffer.

The old furnace would need to be replaced soon. When her dad replaced it the last time he went for the cheapest option, just like everything else in his life. He'd almost lost the shop when his customers noticed the drop in quality, but Josie had won them back when she took over. They knew her and trusted that she remembered how things used to be.

She did remember. She remembered how it felt to sit in the kitchen and watch her grandfather and her mother stretch molten sugar to make peppermint sticks. She remembered the first time she and her sister were allowed to make little marzipan mice for the Christmas window display. She remembered all the different scents of the shop, anise and lemon, cinnamon and chocolate, burnt sugar and scorched pine nuts. The good and the bad, she loved them all.

Some of the customers she didn't love. "I'm sorry, Mrs Davidson, the praline will be another fifteen minutes or so. Can I get you a cup of coffee while you wait?" They didn't sell coffee—Caramella wasn't a café—but sometimes a cup from their personal stash went a long way toward appeasing annoyed customers.

Mrs Davidson scowled at her, but nodded and stood aside for the next customer. Josie handed the counter over to Bianca, who appeared just in time, and retreated to the kitchen to pour two coffees from the fresh pot. Despite her manner, Mrs Davidson was one of their best customers, regularly buying pounds of marzipan, praline, and marshmallow for her cake shop across town. They had a deal and neither sister was going to jeopardize it for the sake of pride.

The second cup was for Josie herself. She took a moment at the kitchen window which looked out, not into an alley as you might expect, but over the Mill River. Three generations of her family had enjoyed this view – her mother had grown up in this very building, in the upper-floor apartment where Josie now lived. Josie's strongest point of pride wasn't her business degree, or the month she spent studying at a French confiserie. Her greatest pride was keeping her grandfather's shop running and bringing it back to the quality he'd insisted on.

She finished her coffee and checked the praline. It was cool enough to process into the small shards Mrs Davidson had ordered, and soon Josie had it packaged up neatly to take out to her. Bianca flashed her a grateful smile when she handed it over, and the shop regained its peace.

Seven other things needed to be done in the kitchen, and an hour later Josie was carefully laying hot tuiles over molds to cool when Bianca came in. "I don't know how you do that," Bianca said for hundredth time. "You must have cast iron hands."

"The trick is to do it quickly."

"I just drop them if I try that."

Josie shrugged and laid down the last tuile. "It's just practice. But you have better things to do."

Bianca was still in school, in the last year of a Master's in chemistry. While Josie had come away from her grandfather's kitchen with a love for combining flavours, Bianca had put everything under a microscope to examine its structure. Josie made candy using recipes and instinct, but Bianca could explain the exact crystalline differences between soft ball and hard ball stage. She just didn't, anymore, because Josie started tuning her out ages ago.

Bianca moaned in reply. "I've got a thing due tomorrow. Can you handle the rest of the afternoon without me?" She was already taking off her apron before Josie could answer.

"Sure. I just have to do the candied citrus."

"Call me if you get slammed when school lets out."

Their best business of the day, by cost at least, came from the elementary school down the street. When classes let out they were flooded with kids, some to spend money, some to just look, but even the browsers eventually came back with a parent to buy. Later on came the teachers, looking for a little something to sweeten a hard day. Every once in a while it would be a parent in the morning, looking for a last minute gift for a favoured (or overworked) teacher. Greg Nichol, whose son was reportedly a hellraiser, came in monthly for a box of fruit jellies.

Josie freely admitted that the kids were her favourite customers. They never hesitated to ask what something was, and their reactions ranged from excitement to outright disgust. It was refreshing, a change from the usual customers who either stuck to old habits and ignored anything new, or who pretended they knew more than she did and refused to take advice. There was very little snobbery involved with the kids; in fact, many of them were better behaved than her adult customers. And every once in a while there would be that one child who wanted to know how the chocolate covering stayed on, or how she got the sugar to look like that, and those were the best. For them Josie was considering offering a few classes on candy-making in the summer. She needed to work it around Bianca's schedule, though, because no way could she manage on her own.

While the citrus peels were cooling in their syrup she put up the "back in five minutes" sign and hopped over to the sandwich shop two doors up. She usually brought lunch down with her, but she hadn't had time to go grocery shopping this week. She rarely bothered to make sandwiches as good as theirs anyway. Unfortunately, her personal budget didn't allow the indulgence often enough.

The phone was ringing when she got back and she barely answered it in time.

"Jo-Jo!" Their cousin Abby was the only person who still called her that, and even though Josie hated it she said nothing because it meant at least she didn't have to ask who was calling. All the women in the family had similar voices and calling could be a nightmare of polite hedging if one person didn't identify herself. "Guess what?"

Josie already knew what, but she pretended she was guessing. "Philippa asked you to marry her?"

Abby sighed heavily. "Mom told you, didn't she?"

"Sorry. She called this morning to ask if I'd do desserts for the wedding."

"I think she called everyone this morning, because so far no one's surprised."

No one would be surprised anyway, because it was obvious they were headed in that direction. "I haven't had a chance to tell Bianca, if you want to call her separately."

"Thanks," Abby said, the spark back in her voice. "And as for dessert, I don't even know what kind of wedding we're having, let alone food. But it is a good idea, so think about it?"

"I've already been plotting in the back of my head. Give me a month's notice, okay?"

"I can try."

A couple of seconds after hanging up, Josie heard Bianca's phone ring upstairs. She felt a little stab of loneliness at the thought that one day it would be Bianca calling her with news. Never mind that Josie would already have lost her to some great job in a different city, it was marriage that seemed like permanently losing her sister. She wished sometimes that she could pick up her shop and move with her, but there were way too many reasons that wouldn't work.

In a weird way she felt like Bianca had her whole life ahead of her, while Josie, exactly the same age, had lived it all and was in a sort of stasis. What did you do after you achieved all your dreams?

The street Josie's shop was on dated back nearly to the founding of the town in the mid-nineteenth century. The building itself, and the others around it, were considerably newer, having been replaced and rebuilt several times. Josie's building, which her grandfather had bought in the fifties, hadn't been renovated since the forties except to replace the old wiring and heating. The building across the street was in worse shape; it probably still had the knob and tube wiring and from what she could see through her living room window upstairs it was missing a lot of plaster.

The old Teufel building was a sore spot in an otherwise lovely and increasingly-gentrified downtown. The shop on the main floor changed tenancy regularly, and few of the businesses increased the street's charm. It had been a debt-collection agency, a telemarketing office, and, most recently, a skeevy used bookstore that even people who loved used bookstores wouldn't go into because of the overwhelming smell of sewage permeating from the goods. The upper floors had burned twice in fifty years, and, people said, were due for another fire any time now. But the building was historically important, so the heritage committee refused to let it be torn down.

Add to that the fact that the building had been for sale for nearly a decade, combined with the rumour of a crack den on the top floor, and the Downtown Business Association was desperate. Jokes about the location being cursed were second-nature now.

So Josie was mildly surprised when a chain link fence appeared around the building with a sign stating that it was under development. The company listed was one that had done an excellent job restoring a few buildings elsewhere in the city, so Josie greeted the news with a sigh of relief and a quick thought to her property value.

"What do you think'll go in there?" Bianca asked when she noticed Josie once again gazing out the front window of the shop.

"If we're lucky it'll be condos." The kind for tech workers who never baked but had the money for good quality treats.

"If not?"

"A bakery. Or some other food shop that smells really great and diverts our walk-ins."

"We'd just do some fancy chocolate sculptures in the window, like Grandpa used to do. That always brought people in."

Yet another tradition Josie's father had ruined, but one that Josie hadn't brought back. "It's probably time to start that up again anyway. I think I still have all his plans somewhere."

"Maybe for Christmas?"

"Or something small for Halloween." A meringue skeleton would be cheap but dramatic. And also simple. Josie didn't have a whole lot of artistic talent. She could pipe an even line and a fair assortment of flowers and leaves, but that was execution rather than creativity.

Bianca seemed to be thinking along the same lines. "Could we afford to hire someone?"

"I'll work up the numbers for holidays and see what we can manage." Josie had seen shops in Paris that changed their window sculptures weekly. She didn't think they could afford that, either in labour or materials. An hour spent sculpting a chocolate ferris wheel no one would get to buy was an hour that could have been spent making sweets that actually brought in money. The chocolate that sat in the window for a week in the shape of a ferris wheel couldn't be melted down to make truffles, at least, not legally. Josie had a horror of violating health codes; in a city like Concordia—where the news felt very small town no matter the population—no one would ever forget.

Later that afternoon when Josie looked out the front window again the construction site was occupied by workers in yellow hardhats and dust was already covering the upstairs windows. Business was slow and Josie had a batch of assorted strudel from a cancelled order that were about to go stale, so she packed them up in a store box, added a note in her best italic, and quickly ran them over to the foreman. She had to hurry back because of course as soon as she left the shop three customers entered.

The next morning there was a note on her door with a thank you and an order for another box, especially the plum, please. She still had some leftover dough, so while it came to temperature she could make up more of the plum filling, absurdly pleased that they'd asked for it specifically; she'd discovered it at a Ukrainian market and though it was her favourite it never sold as well as the maple-apple or raspberry-filled.

Just after two a man in jeans and workboots came in. He was absurdly handsome, blond hair greyed by plaster dust, dark eyes sparkling with humour, cheekbones like Josie only wished she had. "Hi. Are you Josefina?"

"Josie, yes."

His hand, when he held it out, was clean; he'd clearly made an effort to wash the dust and god knows what else off his hands and face before entering her shop. She appreciated that. "I'm Dave. I'm here to pick up the pastries, if they're ready."

"I just boxed them up about ten minutes ago." She brought out the box and put it on the counter. "A dozen is enough? I have more if not."

"That's good. There's only six of us right now."

"A dozen at two-fifty each is thirty dollars. Tax is included in the price."

He laughed, but pulled out his wallet. "Someone else is going to have to pay tomorrow." He had a great smile to go with his great cheekbones.

Josie was just a bit smitten. She folded a small paper menu and slipped it into the side of the box. "I have cheaper treats, too. But let me know by the end of the work day if you want more of these." She tapped the paperboard lid. "They're a little time intensive."

"Why, thank you, Josie."

"You're welcome, Dave." He didn't seem eager to leave, so she ventured a question. "I'm thrilled to see you're renovating the hellhole. Any idea what's going in there when it's done?"

He shook his head. "Can't tell you. We signed all kinds of NDAs before starting work."

"Wow. Must be important."

"It's a big customer, all right."

"Well, I can't wait to find out who it is."

"You'll be surprised, I know." His smile weakened; it was just a flash, but enough for her to notice. He turned away before she could pin an emotion on him and went out the door without another glance.

2

Simon's revenge, he'd tell his friends later, was a stroke of genius, a precursor to his later success at, well, everything, but mostly deviousness.

His mom had business at the candy shop—he couldn't remember later what she went in to buy, and she didn't even remember the day in question—and he entertained himself by watching Josie's grandpa make chocolate Santas.

"Would you like to see?" the old man asked him, and he beckoned Simon back behind the counter.

Simon stood on his tiptoes until Mr Fabrizi slid a stepstool out from under the counter.

"See we have two different pieces, front and back." He showed Simon, who nodded. They were definitely front and back of Santa. "Then we take some more chocolate," he dipped a wooden stick, like a Popsicle stick, into a bowl of melted chocolate, "and make sure we cover all the edges. Then we glue them together, like this." He put the pieces together and then wiped off all the extra melted chocolate. "Then we put them aside to cool."

Simon looked at the bowl of chocolate, and looked at the hollow insides. "Can you put some chocolate inside them?"

The old man nodded. "We could, but that particular chocolate will become hard when it cools. Better would be to put soft caramel or thinned marzipan. Then the whole Santa's not too hard to bite."

Simon's mother called him, then, and he thanked the old man for showing him the Santas.

It turned out his mother had bought a whole box of the hollow Santas. "Those are for taking to school," she said. "For your Christmas party next week."

As an adult telling the story, Simon would laugh at this point. "So you can see how the train of thought goes: I have to give a hollow chocolate Santa to the kid who stole my candy at Halloween. Hollow chocolate Santas can be filled with something. What can we fill it with? Well, there was a whole bottle of bright green dish soap on the counter."

Five-year-old Simon could picture the soap bubbles floating out of Josie's mouth when she talked after eating the Santa, and that was funny enough to try. So he took the pointiest thing he could find ("A screwdriver, I think") and put a hole in the Santa at the bottom, where no one would look. Then he poured in the soap ("Mom blamed my sister for the soap all over the floor").

But how would he keep it from dribbling out? White glue. But the white glue was white, and you could see it. So he found a brown marker and coloured in the glue. Then he put it back in the tray, right at the bottom so he'd remember to give it to the right person.

"She cried. It was pretty funny. Then she hit me for laughing at her."

Simon was not strictly happy to be home. He was elated to be back in Concordia; he'd missed the narrow streets and the buildings no more than twelve stories high. You could stand anywhere in downtown and still see trees, even if they were in the hills on the outskirts. He'd always felt stifled in big cities, so when he got the chance to come back he took it without even thinking.

Which was pretty much his problem. He hadn't been thinking when he asked for the Concordia project. He must have been distracted when the architects presented the final plans; he hadn't noticed the exact intersection on River Street. It was ten kilometres long and his mental map was mostly a blur.

All he'd wanted was to get back home for a little while to take care of his mom.

So now he stood outside the renovation site that would be the first boutique retail centre of

Caldecutt Candies and stared across the road at the darkened storefront of Caramella, Josefina Rutherford, prop.

He really hadn't been thinking.

The gold lettering on the window glared back at him, her name popped out in a slightly different shade to the rest. The store had been there for nearly sixty years, and who was he to drive it out of business? What gave him the right?

To be completely honest, he'd forgotten. He remembered Josie, of course. He remembered her pranks and her grandfather and walking past the store after school every day, and that one memorable day, on the way to school. But how could he have forgotten that she took over? That she'd always dreamed of making the shop her own? Or maybe he never knew she'd succeeded. Maybe he mistook her for Bianca; it's not like it hadn't happened before.

Not that he would have knowingly done this to Bianca, either. She was a sweetheart, as smart and sneaky as her sister, but unfailingly nice. She'd helped him with his math homework more times than he would admit, uncaring of the perpetual state of war between him and Josie.

When Simon first suggested Concordia for the project he hadn't researched it much, assuming it hadn't changed. But the tech sector had moved in when he wasn't looking, giving the downtown neighbourhoods a liveliness they hadn't seen since the last department store closed two decades ago. His mother still talked about downtown like it was a rundown wreck of broken windows and sidewalk junkies. He hadn't had reason to go there when he visited at holidays, and she'd never mentioned the factories-turned-incubator spaces, the condos going up where parking lots had been, the new restaurants, boutique grocers, and clothing shops. Not that there were many, especially on River Street where his project was, but they were steadily encroaching. The city council was even talking about putting in bike lanes.

A warm light shone in an upper window, and he wondered if they still had the apartment there on the second and third floors. He'd been in there a couple of times with Bianca, amazed that they fit so many people in such a small space. He and his parents had a big house outside of town, just the three of them and his sister. His mom still lived there.

He hadn't told her either, that he was in town. If he did, the news would be all over the place within a day and it wouldn't take even that long for someone to make the connection. Right now NDAs were the only thing protecting his ass from the might and wrath of Josefina.

Did he dare cross the street? If Josie was anything like her grandfather she'd started work in the kitchen at least an hour ago, prepping for the early-morning crowd. If she came out and saw him gawking in her window, well, he'd never make the meeting with the foreman, that was for sure. But it looked like she'd brought back Taddeo's window decorations; he could see fall colours, but couldn't make out any figures.

He dared, cutting across the road out of sight of the shop window and sneaking up on it from the side. His laugh almost gave him away when he saw the farm scene, complete with rickety house made from sponge toffee and colourful sugar glass leaves scattered over the lawn. The trees looked like painted fondant and the animals were cookies. If they tasted as good as they looked she might be driving his store out of business, not the other way around.

A light came on in the store, then another, and he had to get to his meeting anyway, so he scuttled back across the street, hoping he looked like just a random guy in a suit.

The sign mocked him several times a day after that, because despite the great progress on the store space, they still weren't done the back stairs, which meant he had to enter and exit from the front. He felt kind of dorky doing it, too, because he'd bought a new toque just to wear to work as a disguise and he kept his scarf wrapped up around the lower part of his face. He should have felt like a spy. Instead, he felt like a felon.

But he liked the work itself, and that couldn't be bad, right? The construction team were great people, open and friendly and willing to share their boxes of pastries if he bought them all coffee, which he was happy to do anyway. Before he arrived they'd ripped up the floors and repaired all the plumbing going out to the city points, which helped immensely with the smell. They'd sistered bad beams, replaced the aluminum wire with copper, and torn out the nicotine-brown plaster. His job was to oversee the operation, to make the necessary last minute decisions and keep the whole thing on budget. It was his first time managing such a project, and he was incredibly glad for the input of the construction team. They were all locals—he was pretty sure Matti had taken Simon's sister to prom—and all invested in making this site a success for the sake of not only their future jobs, but their city as a whole.

And he was glad for that, even though it wouldn't be quite as much of a boost to the downtown as he'd thought when he first proposed building there. So he suppressed the nagging part of his brain that hated when retail juggernauts took over neighbourhoods and drove out the small businesses, the part that thought gentrification was a bad word, only allowing it out during the lonely evenings in his hotel room, when he often spent time figuring out how they could give more than just a few retail jobs to the community.

Simon kept busy for the next week. He drove his mom around and spent weekends doing small chores; chores she needed to have done and he needed to keep from thinking about how he was about to tank his relationship with his most interesting childhood friend.

But hadn't he done that when he first moved away from Concordia? He'd been so eager to get out of what he'd thought was a grimy little city of no value that he hadn't bothered to keep in touch with any of his classmates. Any news was passed through his mother, and these last few years there'd been little of even that.

So many things he'd assumed would be better in Toronto—better indie cinemas, more neighbours to chat with, more access to culture in general—and they were for a while, but the city got more expensive and people got busier and more paranoid and those little facets of home disappeared. And now he looked at Concordia with new knowledge; it was a great city that could support an indie cinema right downtown, where you could walk down the street and see buildings named after your great-grandfather's boss. Where you knew the name of your great-grandfather's boss because you were in band with his great-great-granddaughter and her mother had shared census records with yours.

So he'd taken the job overseeing the renovation and installation of Caldecutt's first retail store as a way of testing how he'd adapt to life in Concordia again, and now the very thing that allowed him to make that decision might very well put him in a kind of hell. Because the people of Concordia loved Caramella and stood by Josie in a way they'd never stood by her father. And that right there, in one sentence, was the fatal flaw of life in small places. If his store caused Josie's to shut down he'd let them lead him to the witch-burning pyre.

As yet no-one except the builders knew what store they were working on, or why he was back in town, and he was going to keep it that way for as long as he could. It would take months to get the building in shape before they could start installing anything identifiable, so he had that long to figure out a way to get himself out of this mess.

3

They weren't in the same class in school anymore, but that didn't mean Josie forgot about Simon's sin against her Grandpa Taddeo's milk chocolate. Recess, lunch, sports club after school were all options when Josie was planning her revenge. She could still taste the soap at times, and made sure to break open all the chocolate bunnies she got the following Easter. She still ate the ears first, but never bit directly into them.

It wasn't until the school picnic that she got back at him. She was watching her friend play with her dog, and the dog stopped to poop, and Josie had the best idea. Simon's baseball glove was right there on the picnic table but he was over at the fountain.

But how would she pick up the poop? It was gross and she didn't want to touch it. She searched the food table for something to use when she saw an even better plan in the form of pats of butter oozing in the sun. She carefully grabbed a handful and slipped them into the glove. Sure that no one had seen her, she sat down again to wait.

She almost missed it because Bianca sprayed her with a water pistol and oh, she was done for.

But she was facing the right way when Simon put his glove on, and close enough to hear his shout and see the look of awesome grossness on his face. It didn't even matter that her distraction let Bianca soak her entire behind with water. Simon looked right at her, and Josie just smiled sweetly and waved.

He didn't retaliate for a whole year. Josie would tell you it was because he lacked spontaneity. Simon would tell you he preferred careful planning to slapdash theatrics.

Things escalated over the next year:

On the first day back to school Simon greased Josie's locker handle with Vaseline.

In retaliation for that, Josie dusted the inside of his ball cap with pink glitter.

Simon wrapped Josie's Princess Jasmine doll, which she had taken to school to show her friends, up like a mummy and hid her clothes behind the bookshelf.

In art class Josie snipped the head off his clay dog so he had to carefully put it back on with wire for firing.

Both remember that year with disgust and fondness.

Simon rolled up to his family home just before eight on Saturday morning. When he'd talked to his mom last night she'd suggested he come over and take her to market for breakfast. Even though he knew he'd be up at six and starving long before eight he'd agreed, because what else did he have to do on a Saturday? And anyway, she'd been raving about the food at this one vendor every time he talked to her lately, so why not try it out?

He'd swear the house hadn't changed a bit since he'd left. It was still a boxy 1970s ranch, red brick with white trim and a door that was olive green when they moved in and had swiftly been painted a proper 90s primary yellow. She repainted the door every once in a while; currently it was a midtone green not far from the olive it once was.

Like the outside, inside only the details changed. Throw rugs, the blanket draped over the back of the couch, the decorative pillow on the armchair, they changed, but the furniture itself and how it was arranged never budged.

His mom was in the kitchen, judging by the cursing. Her Saturday morning ritual included attempting the newspaper crossword puzzles and getting frustrated by her own assumptions.

"Can you believe this?" she said, holding the folded paper up. "They misspelled pearl."

Simon took the paper and followed the tip of her finger. She'd written in "pear" and added an L to the end, graphite shiny over the black ink. He checked the clue, then the answer, which was "purl". He'd long ago grown tired of correcting her, so he let her have her pointless anger. Better she be angry at a puzzle than at herself again.

"Come on," he said instead. "Show me these amazing pies."

At the door he pulled his boots back on and waited while she wrapped herself up in coat and scarf. She always seemed to be cold now, cold and angry and aged beyond her years since his father died of Covid-19.

In the car they talked about the usual things: the hotel the company put him up at, what he was reading, had he seen any of his high school friends again? "And of course you'll come with me to Alyssa's for Halloween," she added after a list of plans for the next month.

He thought he'd misheard her, that maybe she meant Thanksgiving, but no, she'd already talked about hosting Thanksgiving herself. "You're going to drive two hours for Halloween?"

She waved her blue-gloved hand. "It's an easy drive, and we'll stay the night."

Simon kept his eyes on the road. This next intersection was tricky, after all. "But why?"

"Because it's Nathan's first time trick or treating. Alyssa wants me there to help give out candy."

He nodded. "Well, she hasn't invited me, and anyway, I've got meetings. If you wait for me to get off work you'll never get there in time."

Simon liked Halloween, but not enough to drive to another city just to see a costume he'd get pictures of anyway.

The market building was in downtown, not far from his work, in a section populated mostly with lunch places of every variety. He'd had jerk goat from one of them a few nights before and was still thinking about going back. Maybe after the hand pies.

Despite her weekly whining, Josie actually liked market days. Her first customers were always the other vendors and they'd usually stop and chat before getting back to their stalls, so she got to meet a variety of people, including many of those she bought fruit and other ingredients from. As well, most of the new people would come her way, and it was always a boost to be told she'd been recommended as the best in the city (hey, it said so on her bakery case) or that they remembered her grandfather.

Her stall was inside, right near the front entry, close to where it had been in his time. Her father hadn't wanted to bother with the early mornings of market, so had given up the stall, one of the many reasons Josie had had to fight to bring the shop back into prosperity. It had been around the same time that the downtown area emptied out, and a lot of people had simply forgotten they existed, or thought they closed down. Luckily, those were the same people who were thrilled to see her running things now.

And this morning she got to see what all the fuss was about in the corner opposite her. The space had been under renovation for nearly two weeks and this morning it had revealed itself to be a second location of the café upstairs, which could only be good for both businesses.

At least market was one place that chain stores would never be allowed to invade.

As usual, market traffic was slow in the early morning, giving Josie a chance to lay out her wares and get herself a cup of coffee and just generally wake up. By eight it picked up as the semi-serious marketers arrived, and after that traffic would keep building as the stragglers who didn't care about crowds or just needed one thing came in. Her best sales period was around nine, as the crowds around the butcher, cheese, and fish vendors thinned out and they all came to her for a restorative treat.

It was around this time that she usually saw Mrs Jeffries. She often came in with a friend or two, always raving about Josie's pastries even though she could never remember Josie's name. And there she was, three customers deep, talking to a short-ish man with a head of soft-looking black curls. The next time Josie was able to see him was when he stepped up to her counter and she really should have seen this coming at some point, but to be fair, a lot of their classmates who left never came back.

"Simon," she said, as pleasantly as she could. "Nice to see you again. And Mrs Jeffries, what would you like today?"

She ordered the cherry hand pie with the vanilla sugar, then stepped aside, saying, "I didn't know you knew Simon."

Simon looked up from examining the case. "We went to elementary school together."

"I didn't know your family had been here that long," she said to Josie.

Simon closed his eyes for a second then replied, "Mum, her family's been here longer than ours. You used to shop at her grandfather's bakery." He pointed to the pumpkin-shaped pastry and nodded.

Josie clacked her tongs together and plucked out a perfectly browned pastry while replying. "Yes. There's a picture of us all right there." She gestured with her head at the framed photo on the counter. She tried to be sympathetic to Mrs Jeffries, to anyone who clearly hadn't made it through the pandemic unscathed, but sometimes it felt like deliberate offence.

Simon picked it up to show it to his mother. It was their whole family; Josie and Bianca and their older brothers, their parents and their mother's parents, all outside the shop window. Josie still had long hair in the photo.

"There you go," Josie said, handing over his treat.

He thanked her with a brilliant smile and asked as he paid, "Where can I get a good cup of tea to go with these?"

She would have offered him a cup from her freshly-brewed pot under the counter, but there were now five others in line behind them and she didn't want to have to field those questions. She pointed to her left. "Over in that corner is a chocolatier. They have a decent variety."

He gave her a thumbs up and got out of the way so she could tend to the rest of her customers. They kept her busy, too busy to think about the shy looks he'd given her, the how softly his hair had grown out, how his oddly deep voice seemed to resonate within her.

She hadn't seen him since they were both twenty-ish. She and Bianca had been celebrating their birthday at the bar near campus and he'd come around their table to say hi. Then he'd left just as abruptly, on his way to a new job in Toronto; something to do with a bank, she thought.

Since then the only times she'd heard about him were from his mother – "my son's coming down for the holiday", or "it was a gift from my son", stuff like that. He'd never come to market before, and he'd never come to any of the big local celebrations that she could tell, anyway.

Why he was here now was a mystery.

She wondered if he'd be sticking around, and for how long.

Bianca held down the shop on Saturday mornings; they both considered it rent for her apartment on the third floor. Josie wouldn't have cared if she couldn't pay rent—the other renter paid Josie's property taxes and the shop was doing well—but Bianca wanted to pay her some way and helping out in the shop was the best thing Josie could think of.

One of the things Bianca did when the store was slow was research classic recipes and figure out how to make them work on a by-the-piece model. They had all of their Grandfather's recipes, but bringing new items in occasionally helped keep their customers happy. Not having to do the adaptation herself kept Josie happy. She loved to experiment in the kitchen, but only with her own ideas, not other people's.

As Bianca wrapped up the latest customer's purchase Josie busied herself by tidying the pastry cabinet – sweeping up crumbs, removing empty trays, wiping fingerprints off the outside. By the time she was done restocking for the afternoon Bianca was already pulling her backpack out of the small storage closet between the kitchen and the shop.

"I'll be late tonight," she said, gathering her jacket from its hook. "We've got to finish that draft then we're going out for dinner."

Josie nodded. "Text me when you're on your way home."

A customer came in, someone new, so Josie didn't wait for Bianca to acknowledge her before turning on her customer service smile.

Simon had never been a coward. He gave as good as he got in the eternal childhood prank war with Josie, he went out of town to university, he talked his way into his current job, and he was going to say hello to Bianca at her cramped, crowded bar table.

Just as soon as he finished his drink.

He also never broke promises, not even to himself, so the moment he swallowed the last amber drop he stood up and crossed the room to her table.

She didn't notice him at first – he could only hope she didn't remember him, but that was a faint hope at best.

"Hi, Bianca."

The whole table stopped talking. Bianca's eyes widened and she put her hand over her mouth. "Simon," she said, muffled by her hand.

And then, to his great relief, she pushed away from the table and hugged him.

"Oh my god, how've you been? What are you doing back? Tell me everything." Her hand went back to her mouth. "Josie's going to flip."

"She knows," he said. "We saw each other at market this morning."

Bianca dragged him to an open table for two and now held a chair for him. "Sit. Talk to me."

He gestured back to the corner they came from. "But what about your friends?"

She shrugged. "Fellow lab rats. We just submitted a paper and came out to celebrate. They'll understand."

So he sat and told her what he'd been doing in the vaguest terms, not actually mentioning his company name. He didn't think the secret had got out, but you never knew.

In turn he learned everything about her studies and the candy shop and Josefina and how she was helping to put Bianca through grad school.

Every time he looked at Bianca, every time she mentioned her sister, his stomach churned. He'd thought he knew what guilt felt like, but this was totally new.

And he wasn't just feeling guilty. He envied how close they were, their family, their legacy. Even Bianca, who had little interest in baking and candy-making, was invested in keeping the shop alive, simply because it was as much family as the people who ran it.

Simon wasn't sure he'd ever felt that kind of loyalty to anything or anyone. Not even his job, which—he'd found out that afternoon—was going extremely well.

"And how're your mum and dad?" he asked, desperate to change the subject away from Josie.

"Excellent, as far as I know. We get weekly postcards – you know they moved to Italy, right?"

He hadn't, but he was glad to hear all about it if it meant he didn't have to talk about himself and what he was doing.

But when he got back to his hotel room he began to wonder why he felt guilty. He hadn't suggested the Teufel building. He hadn't had any say in the location. They could have chosen Stratford or Milton or Orangeville. They could have chosen the mall on the other end of Concordia or that old grocery store right between the universities.

And he'd seen the traffic Josie's shop got; there was no reason to worry about its health. No one who could afford her prices would stoop to buying from Caldecutt's, so he was doing the community a favour in providing a cheaper alternative.

There was no reason for him to feel guilty about doing his job well.

The run-up to Thanksgiving was always a little rushed. Josie didn't make large pies—there were plenty of proper bakeries around that did that—but she did make custom edible centrepieces and party trays as well as gift assortments.

It was also the beginning of colder season sweets – the ginger cookies and spiced shortbread, the boozy truffles and maple sugar. It meant choosing new recipes based around whatever was trending and designing new name cards for the display. She also had to practice her sugarwork more – the shards in the window pretending to be fallen leaves were good enough, but she wanted better for her customers' homes.

At least they'd got the window done on the first of October, so she didn't have that on top of it all.

She was fixing one of the chairs when the door opened, her grandfather's little bells tinkling in harmony alerting her, giving her time to stop her work just as Simon entered. He didn't see her at first, so she could watch him for a moment as he smelled the candying peel, cinnamon and nutmeg, chocolate. He looked like that sweet kid again as he smiled, perhaps at the same memories she had.

"Simon," she called as she levered herself up off the floor. She set the chair to one side where no one would use it, then dusted her hands off and headed behind the counter. "What can I do for you?"

He shrugged, stepping farther into the store, raising his voice to be heard over the tap running. "I wanted to say hi properly, I guess. I'm going to be in town for a while, so, yeah."

Josie dried her hands off before turning back to him. "I'm glad to hear that. We should hang out sometime." She gestured at the display case. "You want something?"

He peered down at his shoes then studied the case. "I want to take my team some goodies." He gestured vaguely as he finished talking.

"So a variety? How much do you want to pay?" Her prices were decent individually, but could get alarming when you stacked up a big order.

He looked a little closer at the offerings. "I'm interested in volume and ease of eating on the job. Those pizzele," he began, and Josie smiled because nobody got out of her grandfather's store without a lesson in Italian pronunciation. "I have five employees right now, so do you think fifteen would be okay?" He finally looked straight at her as he spoke.

"I think that'd be fine," she replied, already putting together the box they'd go in. "They're all orange-flavoured."

"Okay? I have no idea. I'm just trying to be a good team leader."

39

"I think they'll go over well." She counted them out by fives into the box, standing on their ends, then sprinkled icing sugar into the crevices, knowing it would drift on the pattern baked into each of them. She closed up the box and brought it over to the till, letting Simon know the price as she did.

Once he'd paid he hovered a moment. "Josie," he said, then stopped.

Josie dropped her customer service facade. "What's up?"

"Nothing," he replied. "It's just good to see you again. I'm glad you're doing well here."

"Thank you. You too."

And he was out the door and she could only go back to her tippy chair with a vague sense of elation.

4

Josie would describe herself at twelve as "Petulant. But I knew what I wanted and I wasn't afraid to ask for it." To which Bianca would add: "And when she didn't get it she'd complain for days."

Thus went the inevitable fights with her mother, the most common being over Josie's hair.

That day her hair was in a thick braid down her back because she hadn't been interested in styling the curls the way Bianca did. "And anyway," she told her mom, right there in the store for the customers to hear, "Grandpa agrees I should cut it short. He says it'll be better for working in the kitchen."

All it took was that single, pointed finger to rile Josie up, let alone what her mother said back. "You're not working in the kitchen until you're fifteen. And Grandpa doesn't get any say in what your hair looks like. You'll keep it long until you're old enough to pay a stylist yourself."

Josie slammed her way out of the shop, Bianca a few steps behind her.

"Does it really matter that much?" Bianca asked, honestly curious.

"It's hot in the summer and hats slide off it in the winter and oh my god it takes way too long to brush." Bianca's hair was straighter, taking more after their father's family. It didn't take hours to blowdry. "And I hate how boring it is."

She saw Bianca's hand go to her own head, but at the moment she didn't care about her sister's precious feelings.

"Everybody has long hair," she continued. "And it's not like it won't grow back."

What she didn't realize was that they'd passed Simon a moment ago, and he trailed behind them, listening, waiting for an idea.

"Maybe," Bianca said, thinking hard, "maybe you could accidentally get gum in it. Then you'd have to cut it off."

"But I don't chew gum."

"Right. And you've worn your hair braided or up every day this month, so if you wore it down tomorrow she'd get suspicious."

Josie had noticed that her mom hid all the scissors after the first time Josie asked if she could cut it. "Exactly. I guess I'll have to wait."

At recess Josie hung upside down from the little kids' jungle gym, bored and uninterested in how the other girls were talking about music and famous people. Her eyes were closed and she felt strange, lightheaded (duh), and kind of outside her body. It was pretty cool. She didn't notice someone creep up on her until she heard the *snick snick* of a scissors at the same time as something tugged at her braid. She flipped down to the ground and as her head cleared she saw Simon standing just out of reach, holding a thick braid of dark brown hair and grinning.

She touched the nape of her neck and grinned back for a second before screaming. The next day she showed up at school with an awesome new pixie cut.

The pranks mostly ended in high school, when Simon's family moved to the suburbs and he went to a school out there. They still saw each other around, of course, but not quite as often. Any pranking had to be limited to evenings and the odd academic gathering.

Both joined the debating teams, Josie because she thought she had a natural advantage being from a loud, argumentative family, and Simon because he hoped it would help him overcome his slight stage fright. Both were correct, but after the first year, they both stayed on the teams because of the little thrill each got when their schools went up against each other.

At the time they'd have said it was hatred. Looking back on it, though….

Work on the building across the street proceeded quickly, fuelling speculation all over town. You could tell something about a person by asking what they thought was going in there. "Whatever it is it'll fail," came the consensus. "Everything always does, including the original hotel."

As it turned out, everyone's guesses were wrong.

Josie saw the sign first, looking out her window one previously fine morning. "Future home of Caldecutt Candies' first retail shop!" The newspaper confirmed it when they sent a reporter—a woman Josie'd had swimming lessons with as a kid—to ask how she felt. No way was Josie going to tell the truth, that she felt utterly sick to her stomach, so she went with diplomacy.

"Concordia needs fresh business investment. We can only hope this is the first in a long list of new businesses," she said. In the ensuing article there was no mention of her stiff smile and clenched fists. "Personally, our customers are loyal, and appreciate the quality and variety that comes from handmade sweets rather than from large, impersonal factories."

Her mom called from Florence the next morning. "Oh, dear. Your grandfather's spinning in his grave right now. But I know you'll do your best by his legacy. You always have."

That did not make her feel better, and she reflexively noted how long it had been since she'd taken flowers to his grave.

But Bianca was avoiding her. As far as Josie could tell she didn't have a reason to, which was even more suspicious. At least she still did her work in the store.

Josie watched her one morning as Bianca filled skeleton mould with meringue for the coming Halloween window. They'd planned it alongside the fall window, and would be turning the pretty little house into a haunted one.

"You know," Josie said, a note of confrontation in her voice, "usually you'd be chatting about school right now."

Bianca's answering glance held more guilt than she was used to seeing from her level-headed sister.

"It's nothing."

Josie sealed up another box of apple cider caramels to take to market. "You can tell me. Didn't we promise when we made this deal that we'd communicate?"

Bianca just smiled sadly. "It's about Caldecutt."

Josie's heart skipped a beat, then she realized that was stupid, there was nothing they could have done already.

"I found myself hoping they'd," Bianca paused and looked at her hands, which had stopped moving. "That they'd drive you out of business so you could come with me when I graduate."

All Josie could do was envelop her in a hug and say, "You're a horrible person and I'm so glad you're my sister."

Bianca's reply was a choked-off laugh and a pat on the back.

She thought about what Bianca said throughout the morning; would it be so bad to pack up and start a shop in another city? It would probably depend on the city. And what happened when Bianca got a different job elsewhere? Would Josie follow her then, having to start from the beginning yet again?

That made no sense. For all anyone knew Bianca would have to move several times before she found a job worth staying in. This was a decision that could wait. If, in a few years, Josie needed to be closer to her twin then she'd decide then. For now she had a business to protect.

During her slow hours she budgeted for the Halloween treat bags she wanted to sell. She wanted to make them special, but also kid-focused, and that was the hard part. But she knew what sold to the kids who came in after school; she just needed to find a way to make them fit the theme. She also made up a tentative budget for a new hire, someone to take over market days, for example. She could do it if she scrimped just a little bit on...something. She hadn't worked out what yet.

When her thoughts stalled her eyes drifted over to the sign, just visible out her front window. It was inevitable, she supposed; the city was growing more popular and the housing prices were still pretty low. That would change, soon, and once more she was glad she owned the building she lived and worked in. She'd hold on to it until the very last moment she could. She loved this place – not just the shop, not just the rooms she lived in, but the whole building with all its Edwardian charm. It would never be torn down—it had earned its historical designation while her grandfather was still alive—so she didn't have to worry about it falling into less respectful hands, but she just could not imagine living anywhere else. She'd tried, during her school years, and while other cities were exciting in unique ways she always felt small in them, like she'd be swallowed up if she wasn't careful.

In Concordia she felt loved. Important. A member of a wide and varied community with tendrils that stretched out all over the world. It was a common feeling, especially among those who'd been born here. You could leave, but coming back again felt special.

But if she did lose the building, her shop, then what was her life here about? She stared at the work site until the school kids started drifting in to look at the display, when she decided there was no point in thinking about it until it happened.

Josie was updating the shop Instagram and about to move on to Facebook when her phone rang. It was the middle of the night for her parents, so it had to be either important or spam. It was Abby, which meant Josie should probably be nervous.

"Hey, Josie," Abby began, her voice quiet and hesitant.

"What's up?"

Abby made a pained noise. "Don't sound like that, please. It's not that bad."

Josie relaxed somewhat. "So the wedding's still on?"

"Yes! I mean, yeah, don't worry about that. In fact, that's why I'm calling."

Josie pulled up a text file on the computer, figuring she'd have to take notes. "Cool. You have plans now?"

"We want to be married on Christmas Eve. It's special to both of us." She hesitated again. "We were thinking about having the wedding in Toronto, but," she stopped with a sigh. "Grandma just had emergency surgery."

Oh shit. "Is she okay?" And why didn't Mom call to tell her?

"She should be fine. Your mom told me to tell you she'll call once they're back home."

Then it clicked for Josie what the "but" was. It was a little amusing though, because, "So you'll get that Italian wedding you always wanted." They'd gone to visit the old country once as kids, and Abby had loved exploring Milan, where their grandparents had been born.

Abby laughed. "Maybe. But yeah, we'll have the wedding there so Grandma doesn't have to travel."

"I can't begrudge you that."

As Abby chatted about the change in wedding plans Josie checked the calendar she'd filled out last week. December 23rd - Christmas party. December 27 - 50th wedding anniversary. Fuck. She could never get there and back and still work.

"Look, I know it's difficult," Abby said, interrupting her thoughts. "It's okay if you can't come."

"I really can't," Josie replied, as apologetically as she could. "I have two parties to cater on just the wrong days. I can't cancel them." But then she realized, "I'll make sure Bianca can come, okay? She needs some vacation anyway, and I'm sure she'd like to see Mom and Dad and the rest of you."

"You sure you don't need her help?"

"I'm sure." She wasn't, but it was the best she could do. Abby had been like another sister to them for a long time, before her family moved to

Montreal in grade ten. "Don't worry about it. You want me to send anything with Bianca?"

"Any chance I can get a hundred truffles?"

She looked at her calendar again. "Sure. What flavours?"

"Half blueberry-Cointreau dark and half cranberry white?"

"My most ridiculously Canadian flavours? Not a problem. You want fifty maple milk as well?"

"Could you? I wasn't sure if I should ask for that many. That would be amazing."

They discussed logistics for a bit—Josie would definitely need an advance to get good blueberries at this time of year and Abby would make sure customs didn't confiscate the truffles—then wedding plans until Abby needed to go call someone else.

Josie settled back into her work, not realizing until she'd mentioned Christmas coming that for the first time in her life she'd be all alone for the holiday. Last year she and Bianca had their parents as well as Gus and Dan for a few days, but Mom and Dad moved to Italy last year and would definitely stay for the wedding, and Gus and Dan had both taken oil jobs in northern Alberta and had already let her know they couldn't come back.

Was there even any point in putting up decorations if it was just her? She looked around the apartment with new awareness, picturing a Christmas without all the usual trappings.

The place hadn't changed much since she was a kid, perhaps since before she was born. Midtone brown wood floor, white trim, great, fine. Sofa, chairs, side tables, and TV stand in amber woods, relics of her grandparents' mid-century redecoration. Eighties updates including pale blue-green walls and Laura Ashley paper border. A nineties area rug of tufted grey. The walls were cluttered with photos of family, of Italy, and oil paintings her grandmother made when she was in art school. Josie had always liked the one of her great-grandmother in front of a swirling, grey-green backdrop.

She'd lived with it like this all her life, little changing; it even smelled the same, an ever-present scent of baking from downstairs, of onions and garlic from the kitchen through the door. It had been her grandparents' living room and now it was hers, but it had nothing of her in it.

She started searching out evidence of Bianca, but aside from a few textbooks and a red blanket on the sofa she was largely nonexistent. Her bedroom upstairs, the one they'd shared as a child, had been made over several times, always to her specifications. This room, however, was a museum. A mausoleum. It had always been their home and yet it never showed a speck of them.

Except for pictures on the wall, they might never have existed.

The lamp in the corner caught her eye, then. It was a brass post with a weird glass table orbiting the centre and a white pleated shade. She grabbed it high up, like she was throttling it, feeling the cold metal against her palm. The shade smelled awful—how had she never noticed?—like old cigar smoke. Her grandfather hadn't smoked, but some of his friends had. They'd come over for card parties on Sunday afternoons while their wives stayed home to cook the roast. She remembered the smell that wafted up the old heating ducts to her room on the fourth floor.

She ran her fingers across the pleats, making a satisfying zipping noise and sending up a cloud of dust. She'd tried to get rid of it, but couldn't find anything she liked to take its place. It was plugged into the main wall switch, so whatever she got would have to light up most of the room. Touching the shade reminded her of a scarf she'd wanted desperately when she was about ten. It was satin, deeply pleated, in a vibrant purple. Every day on her way home from school she'd go into the hat shop and play with the scarf, running her fingers over the pleats, slipping it over the backs of her hands. Oddly, there weren't a lot of things she remember wanting. Not objects. She let Bianca dictate all their possessions, even through high school when she was more likely to be collecting programmable calculators than clothes. The memory stuck in her throat, choking her.

The scarf had been sold, but not to Josie. Its simple beauty had never come into her house, yet this lamp, this abomination of design was still here after forty years. She unplugged it from the wall and throttled it yet again, determined to get it out of her sight. If she had to read by candlelight for the next month she would, damn the thing. For one brief moment she longed to toss it out the window, but there were people down there who might be hurt, so she dragged its heavy base across the rug until she hit bare wood, then picked it up and carried it out the door, down two sets of stairs, and out the back. One good heave sent it into the trash.

Back upstairs she reconfigured a few lights from other rooms to take up the work and already the room looked substantially different. Bianca would be surprised when she got home, and Josie would have to invite her to get rid of something she hated, too. She suspected they'd spend the evening peeling off the wallpaper border, if nothing else.

She had actually been looking forward to redecorating, and was a little disappointed when the president of the Small Business Association called her for an emergency meeting. The disappointment turned to gratitude when she saw the white board at the front of the room, all decorated up with curlicues and the words "Save Josie's Bakery".

She didn't even try to hold back tears as she greeted the president, Ekua, with an enormous hug. "Thank you," she gasped into Ekua's shoulder. "It means so much to me."

Ekua rocked her a bit, patting her back. "I'd want you all to help me if some big chain African restaurant—" she stopped and pulled away from Josie, "pardon me while I laugh— came in and tried to take my livelihood."

"And right across the street from you!" added Ekua's husband from her side. "They couldn't have put it out by the university?"

Josie slid out of Ekua's arms, but kept hold of one of her hands. "Maybe it will drive the university traffic to my store?"

He grasped her arm, his hand warm and solid. "We can only hope. Now, when are you going to have some West African sweets we can buy?"

It was a common joke, but this time she had an answer for him. "I'm working on it, but you all put peanuts or chilis in everything! I can't keep my customers like that. How about some kokoro? You should come do some quality control tasting for me."

He grinned, teeth bright against his dark skin. "I await perfection. Now, I have to go. We're still serving dinner."

"Thank you, Joseph."

A few more downtown business owners filtered in before Ekua called the meeting to order. Everyone had heard the news by now; the downtown area was still on its upward trend of rehabilitation, so rents were low and small businesses thrived there, and even the ones who weren't in the downtown core didn't want the same thing happening in their neighbourhoods. Everyone had watched as all the local hardware stores and pharmacies died out when the big chains moved in.

If Josie had ever considered moving her shop to a bigger city where she could charge more she must have been deluded because these were her people, even the ones who asked why she sold candies with "weird" spices in them, wouldn't she sell more of the "normal" kind? They were here to support her, that was what mattered right now.

After the meeting, as she always did, she stopped in the middle of the footbridge over the river and leaned forward over the railing, watching the water move under her. She dropped a candy—lemon this time—and made a wish, listening for the plop as it hit the water, just like Grandpa had taught her.

"Thank you," she whispered, completing the ritual.

Footsteps creaked on the bridge to her left, but she ignored them until a figure paused to lean on the rail beside her.

"Keeping up your granddad's rituals, eh?"

She smiled up at the elderly grocer. "It doesn't hurt."

He nodded, then tossed something she couldn't see properly into the water. They both watched the ripples form then die away. "It doesn't at all," he said. "You do it every time?"

"Mostly."

"Good. I was hoping to talk to you," he added, straightening up.

She matched his posture, waiting for him to continue.

"I thought I might start carrying more local products. We already have some produce, but I thought we might expand into sweets."

Through a grin, Josie replied, "I think we could work something out."

"Good." He nodded briskly at her and continued past her towards River Street.

She finished her walk home feeling like maybe she and Bianca and her grandfather's legacy might just be all right.

Simon knew he'd been right to move back when he ended up taking over cooking the Thanksgiving dinner from his mom. He'd really had no idea how hard Long Covid had hit her until now; somehow the last few holidays he'd been home she'd managed, but now she dithered in the middle of the kitchen, unsure of which pot or pan she needed to deal with first.

He clasped his hands on her shoulders and gently said, "Go sit and take a break. I'll take care of things. It's just watching and stirring right now, right?"

She nodded briskly. "Right." He watched her leave and then dove to turn down the burner under the pot of potatoes about to boil over.

His sister and her family would be here soon and then Mom would be occupied with her grandkids. He and Alyssa could finish dinner.

When Alyssa arrived he was checking the temperature on the turkey and trying to decide if he should take it out. It only had a couple more degrees to go so he took it out and tented it, leaving it to cook itself that little bit more on the counter.

"Hey, what's up?" Alyssa said, coming to his side.

He hugged her hard. "It's good to see you."

"I'm so glad you're home." She let go of him. "You are staying, right?"

He started the burner under the potatoes then moved away. "I hope so. I need to find a new job, first, but that might wait until this project is done." And if Caramella didn't go under. If that happened he'd never be able to show his face in Concordia again.

Alyssa might be able to help there, but he'd save that conversation for after dinner.

"You want me to start on the dressing?" she asked, already washing her hands.

"Please. It needs to go in the oven soon."

As they worked they chatted, conversation only broken by his niece and nephew coming in to ask questions, one of which was, "Can we visit your candy store tomorrow?"

He sat down on the floor to get to their height. "Well, my store isn't open yet – it doesn't even have counters yet. But if your mom says it's okay we can go to her favourite candy store just across the street."

Alyssa nodded, probably already planning to fob the kids off on him and take the afternoon to herself. "You can buy me a surprise," she said, confirming his thoughts.

Mollified, the kids ran off. "How did Josefina take the news?" She still stuttered a little over Josie's name, even after all these years.

Simon shrugged, staring more intently than necessary at his hands while he chopped carrots. "I wasn't there when she found out."

"She must have said something to you about it, it being your project."

He scraped the carrot coins into a bowl and picked up the garlic. "She doesn't know that part."

"She's going to be pissed."

"That's why I haven't told anyone."

"You'd better do it soon. Better she hear it from you and not Mom."

She had a good point. "But I'm not doing it tomorrow. The niblings don't need to hear that kind of language."

"Well, tell her I said hi, anyway?"

"Sure."

After dinner he suggested a long walk to Alyssa, so they grabbed their jackets and hats and he led her out across the road to the nearby hiking trail. "I need your help," he said when they hit bare dirt.

"Okay." Alyssa sounded dubious. "What kind of help?"

"You know what you said about Josie earlier? I don't want to hurt her. I don't want to fuck up her business. But I got myself into this position and I have to live with it. You got any advice?"

Alyssa pulled a yellow maple leaf from a tree as she passed, crumpling it in her hand. "Aside from tell her soon?"

"Preferably, yes."

"If I know anything about this town there's going to be a protest against your company and the possibility of displacing downtown businesses. Get in on that."

"If I do that I won't have a job anymore."

"Then I don't know what to tell you. Just try to get ahead of the damage and practice saying you're sorry."

Later, on his way back to the hotel, he started making plans.

The moment Thanksgiving was over Josie devoted herself to Halloween, and she had to give Bianca credit for the window, especially the part about making half of it face inside the shop so people had to come in to see the whole thing.

Once they were in it was hard to leave without buying a little something. Josie even got two orders for catering local Halloween parties, one adult, one children's. She'd needed some creative guidance for those, but the internet was a goldmine of ideas – she just had to adapt them to her recipes and skills.

Catering wasn't what she'd intended when she took over the business, but this wasn't her grandfather's world anymore. Anyway, she didn't think he'd mind. If he were still alive he'd probably just be happy her name was on his shop window.

She had other plans, too, which meant she'd have to start baking sugar cookies soon. She'd met a teacher from down the road at a party in the summer and they'd come up with a plan for her to bring her grade two class in to decorate Halloween cookies. All Josie had to do was make the cookies using the cutters Hannah would buy, and whip up some coloured icing. Hannah would bring the kids and a variety of toppings for the cookies. If it went well Josie would start offering open classes before other holidays, so any parent could bring their kid in. She wouldn't go so far as booking birthday parties, though, because that would probably end up taking over most of her business and frankly, just the thought of making dozens of sugar cookies every week was boring.

So boring that she decided to get it over with. The kitchen was due for a deep clean anyway, might as well make the dough when she was certain she had an allergen-free space. Then she could freeze it and not have to think about it until it came time to bake.

Simon rubbed his hands together and cursed himself for forgetting his gloves. He came back here in October, how could he have neglected his winter gear? It wasn't like he lived somewhere tropical; Toronto got its fair share of snow and freezing temperatures. But somehow he'd missed gloves.

The fair trade shop was warm, thank god, and already decked out for fall with a full selection of winter knitwear, so at least he wouldn't have to go to the mall across town. He'd picked out a pair of rough wool mittens in an oatmeal colour with green stripes and was just turning to buy them when he stopped short before crashing into a familiar figure.

Josie's eyes smiled at him from over her mask, and he wondered how it happened that a utilitarian object could serve to focus such beauty. "Hi, Simon. Good to see you again."

"You, too." Why was he suddenly tongue-tied? He was starting to understand Alyssa, now.

"I wasn't expecting you still be here."

"I'm working here for a while," he said.

"Cool," she replied, taking a step past him. "You should come by the shop."

He toyed with the tag on the gloves. "You think so?"

Josie nodded. "Yeah. I'd like to get to know the new, adult Simon."

"I've got time right now." He started toward the cash desk, Josie following.

"Perfect. Business is kind of slow today, anyway."

As Josie paid for her earrings Simon perused the wares on the counter, the basket of woven toys, the little squares of slavery-free chocolate, the bamboo clipboard with a petition on it? A petition, it seemed, to drive Caldecutt out of town before they even opened. There were already a couple of dozen signatures. If he'd been there alone he would have asked about it, tried to find out who was behind it. It was kind of his job, after all. But Josie was right beside him, so he signed it instead, a deliberately unreadable scrawl next to his not-so-neatly-printed (and maybe a bit misspelled) full name.

As they walked back to the shop, he paused to take in the window display, which had changed since he'd passed by that morning.

It had been a bright collection of red and yellow glass sugar shards scattered around a house, but now the shards had been sprayed black and covered in icing cobwebs, and the previously cheerful house was undoubtedly haunted. They'd roughened it up, making it look derelict, then infested it with marshmallow ghosts. It was surrounded by little vignettes of meringue skeletons digging each other up and a tentacled licorice monster climbing out of an iridescent fabric river. A small sign told people to come in and vote for their favourite scene.

"Did you do all this?" he asked, crouching down to better see the painted details on the trees.

"Don't sound so surprised," she replied as she pulled open the door. The little bell rang over Simon's protest.

"I'm not surprised. I'm impressed."

"Bianca did a lot of the work."

Bianca's head popped out from the kitchen at the mention of her name.

"Oh, it's just you," she said as they entered, with a smile that erased the harshness of the words. She turned back to the kitchen, leaving Simon alone with Josie, who had rounded the counter.

He took a look at the display case. It had changed a lot since her grandfather's time, no longer bare and utilitarian. Now the trays were candy-coloured plastic covered in whimsical paper and little cards named all the treats, which were not entirely Italian anymore. Some German and French had crept in, as well as a few names he thought might be Slavic.

Unlike the case, the wall behind Josie was still decorated in Mr Fabrizi's taste, which ran to photos of cryptids. Simon almost laughed when he saw the local river monster from the 1890s, which had turned out to be plant matter piled up against a rock.

Josie caught him staring at them and smiled. "I couldn't let them go. Sometimes his belief was inspiring." She put a couple of plates on the counter. "Did you know he chose Concordia because of the river monster?"

"Really?"

"He said he liked a little mystery in his homes."

Simon glanced at the photo again. "But they figured it out."

Josie just shrugged. "He never believed it."

Bianca came out of the kitchen with a tray of mugs that smelled like coffee.

"Pick something out," Josie said as Bianca set her tray down on one of the small tables that lined the opposite wall.

He studied the case again, undecided. "These are new," she said, pointing to a tray of what looked like leaf-shaped egg tarts. "They're plum and vanilla custard in a rye pastry."

He mentally shrugged. Why not? "Sure, I'll have one of those."

She handed him his pastry and then came out from behind the counter with two more plates and a stack of Florentines, clearly expecting him to follow her to the table.

Bianca had already handed out coffee, so he took one of the chairs and bit into the pastry not knowing what to expect. What he got was a buttery, earthy, cookie-like base with rich plum jam, a hint of something floral, and sweet custard with a crunchy layer of caramelized sugar on top.

"What do you think?" Josie said, and he could see a hint of nervousness around her mouth.

"It's amazing," he replied with a nod.

Bianca snagged a Florentine and bit into the chewy confection. "Good. It's a new recipe for winter. Josie modified the original but tried to keep the feel of it."

For just a second he considered cracking a joke about the pastry being poisoned, but suppressed it. This new aspect of their relationship—actually maybe becoming friends—was too delicate to risk. Especially with what he knew was coming.

He had to tell them. He knew it was the right thing to do, much better than letting them find out some other way, after they'd rebuilt some trust. But if he did it now he'd probably never be able to set foot in this shop again. So he drank his coffee and ate Florentines that were exactly how they ought to be and answered their questions.

How was his mom? And Alyssa?

Had he seen the new library renovations yet?

"Can you handle kids?" Josie asked out of the blue.

Bianca cackled. "Don't answer that," she said."

But Simon felt like he was being targeted, and he wanted to know why. "I like hanging with Alyssa's kids."

Josie watched him seriously for a moment. "Next Monday I have twenty schoolkids coming to decorate cookies and I need another pair of hands. Can you help?"

It was a test, he knew it instinctively. "Let me know what time and I'll check my schedule."

The conversation moved on, to Bianca's studies, their parents' move, and their mom's new job teaching painting in Florence.

And somehow his job, the reason he was back home, never came up and he couldn't find a sufficient reason to bring it up. So he left feeling like he'd created something new with them, but also feeling like a coward.

5

The day came and Josie was ready. She looked over the list on the counter, trying to memorize the children's names. Twenty of them were on their way, probably in costumes. She had a stack of sugar cookies in spooky shapes, twenty little stations with small pastry bags filled with white, orange, and purple icing, enough sprinkles and little candy shapes to float her cash register, and the desperate hope that it would be enough.

One of the parents—Taslima's dad—had warned her that his daughter was very particular and hated to make a mess. With some consultation from him and Taslima Josie had flooded the cookies with royal icing a few days ahead so they could dry. That way she, and any other child who wanted to, could add smaller patches of colour without worrying about edges.

The fee for this fun afternoon would certainly cover all her time, tools, and ingredients, but she'd still have to clean up afterwards.

Bianca couldn't help, as someone had to deal with customers, so Josie had recruited the help of Emma, one of her part-timers, who made lovely truffles and definitely knew how to change tips on a piping bag. Her other helper was Simon.

He was already here, on the other side of the store checking each child's supply station against a list she'd given him. She left off studying the list and studied him instead. In high school he'd been cute, the object of more than one girl's attention, but now he'd grown into his sharp cheekbones and long eyelashes. His face and body had filled out, softening his lines, making him look more approachable. He'd cut his hair since the last time she saw him, and now it was short enough that she saw little hint of the curls that had taunted him through elementary school.

Rippling thigh muscle showed even through his heavy jeans, and although his arms were pretty normal, his back under his grey t-shirt looked sturdy. Strong enough to pick her up and... stop that, Josie.

He glanced up at her questioningly and she was saved by the arrival of a group of monsters and superheroes and cartoon characters she didn't recognize.

"Masks up!" she called out as the door swung open.

She greeted the kids as Simon ducked into the kitchen to tell Bianca it was time for her to take over the till.

The two-hour session went fairly smoothly. Several kids needed to tell her a story about a tentacled sea monster right now, but only one glitter fight had broken out and most of the kids understood her instructions to only use a little bit of icing at a time or else you'll have to leave them here until tomorrow. A couple she'd had to put under the warmer for a minute but those belonged to kids who didn't care if the icing smudged as long as they got to take pictures first. She hadn't planned to, but Josie ended up taking pictures of all of them with her good camera. She'd email them to Hannah and then hopefully use them to advertise.

Even with how easy the afternoon itself was Josie and Simon were exhausted by the end of clean-up. They collapsed at one of the rear tables, and only then did Josie realize that Bianca was gone. She checked the time, remembering then that Bianca had a meeting at the university.

It should have been time for Simon to go, too, for Josie to lock up the shop and maybe make some dinner, but she didn't want him to leave. She didn't want to leave him. They'd worked so well together today.

"You want a beer?" she asked him.

"Sounds good." He looked her over, noticing her obvious fatigue. "If you tell me where they are I can get them."

"Thanks," she said, letting her head fall to the tabletop. "In the kitchen on the left as you go in is a small fridge where we keep our private stash."

She listened to him leave, the squeak of the fridge door, and his steps coming back before a brown glass bottle thunked in front of her. She managed to raise her head enough for a bracing sip. "Thanks," she repeated.

"No problem."

"I'm glad you're here," she said, then sat up because this was important. "Not just for today, but for good, maybe."

He smiled, glancing down at his hands on the table. "I'm glad too." When he looked back up he met her eyes and her heart actually fluttered, warmth flooding through her at his gaze. She didn't look away but watched him, steady and sure.

The air thickened around them, grew warm, and Josie was glad for how small the café table was, how the chairs were already on the same side, how Simon leaned towards her as they continued to talk. To flirt.

He smiled more often like this, cozy and alone, tired from the work and just a little from the beer. Their conversation drifted to the subject of relationships, other people they'd seen. What they did and didn't like.

Tempted, so tempted, Josie slipped her free hand to Simon's knee and he covered it with his own hand, chilled from the bottle. His skin warmed quickly on hers.

Metal rattled as the furnace came on, startling them both. "Does it always do that?"

Josie took a last swallow of beer before nodding. "It's fine. It's just a loose duct. It can wait for spring."

Simon peered out the window into the dark. "It's windy and snowing a bit. I should get back to the hotel before it gets too bad out there."

She followed him to the door, unwilling to lose what she'd just discovered. "See you soon?" she asked.

"Absolutely," he replied, and his smile could have powered one of her ovens.

At seventeen Simon was kind of a dick, he'd be the first to admit, although he'd follow it up with how most seventeen-year-olds were dicks, Bianca included.

But Bianca had always been nice to him, no matter his relationship with her sister, so really, how could he have known?

He was very, very careful not to outright blame Bianca, even though it was her lie that started the evening off.

You see, he'd been calling Josie. The last time they saw each other, at the busker festival, she'd smiled at him, and not in a mean way, so he'd thought maybe she'd be willing to bury the hatchet and dance on its grave. And he knew she wanted to go to the summer music festival, so he figured why not ask?

It was after school and Josie would be working, so he called the shop phone.

"Caramella."

"Josie?"

"Simon?"

He'd been thrilled when she said yes to his offer of music and ice cream, not so thrilled when Bianca showed up instead.

"Sorry?" She said with a wince. "Josie and I are fighting and I thought it would be funny."

Simon almost walked away, but he liked Bianca too, so why not go with her? It was too late to rearrange with Josie anyway.

He wasn't surprised when they had a great time together. He was surprised that later, in a dark part of the park, she kissed him and they got off together, fully clothed in the grass.

And he was only mildly heartbroken when Bianca told him after that she thought they were better as friends. He certainly hadn't expected her to tell Josie about the whole thing, including the mistaken identity.

He really hadn't expected Josie to cry when she found out.

At this point in the story Josie would hop in, saying, "It took me a couple of years and a lot of distance to trust Bianca completely again."

"And what about me?" Simon would ask.

And she'd grin wickedly for their audience and reply, "You've had your punishment."

They don't really talk about Josie's revenge for Simon going out with Bianca, except to say that it was university and the dorm party was kind of wild and how did he expect Josie to pass up such temptation?

And anyway, it wasn't the act itself that was retaliatory. Telling him about it? That was merely proportional response.

6

The decorations in downtown were changing, but not because of Halloween, Simon realized. The signs in every window said Shop Local. While he was out doing so he saw posters on every corkboard exhorting people to buy their treats at Josie's this Christmas.

All natural, they said.

Fair trade ingredients.

Environmentally friendly packaging.

No palm oils = no destroyed ecosystems.

Handmade. Customizable. Bring your own tins if you desire.

Delivered to your door this holiday season.

Fair pricing.

Winner of Concordia News Best Confectionery 2019 2020 2021 2023

"Really effing delicious", someone had scrawled across one of the posters.

The more he saw around town the more he felt like a complete asshole. Caldecutt was the most popular Canadian candy company, known for their quality and variety, available in grocery and other stores everywhere. A box of assorted chocolates cost half what the same number of

Josie's chocolates would, and a third of that for Caldecutt to produce.

A seventy-year old business, the pride of three generations of Josie's family, could all be destroyed within a few months of Caldecutt opening. Nothing could stop it, and it would be entirely his fault.

He had to tell Josie. He had to do it soon, before their tenuous friendship became solid. Before they acted on all the promise of last evening. Because he was pretty sure that she was it for him; she'd somehow always been in the back of his head.

So he had to tell her before it would be real betrayal. And because he wasn't a coward.

He picked a local café to sit in, one that was busy enough to prove it was good. Coffee in front of him, taste still bitter in his mouth, he texted Josie.

Can I take you out for dinner tonight? I want to tell you something.

He sipped his coffee and waited, then noticed the sign on the display case: Treats provided by Caramella.

He couldn't escape it. His phone dinged the generic notification.

Sounds good. 7pm okay?

He felt a deeply stupid sense of relief, similar to the time he'd asked her out in high school. That had been an attempt at a date. This was not, could not be a date. Not until he'd told her the truth.

7 pm at 158 River. See you then, he replied. Then he stuffed his phone in his pocket again specifically so he wouldn't just text her his secret right now to get it out of the way.

Josie dumped blocks of chocolate in the grater and wondered if she'd just made a huge mistake. Was he going to humiliate her? Leave her there with the bill? Show up with Bianca and humiliate them both?

Or was this a date?

Over the years she'd heard when he came back to town, even if she never saw him, and she always spent his visit waiting for the other shoe to drop. For him to get the final blow in their childhood war. And even now, though they'd spent a few good hours together, she couldn't stop wondering what form his revenge would take.

It would have to be epic.

She started up the grater, hoping the noise would drum those thoughts out of her head. The scent of toasting hazelnuts filled the kitchen as well, and she turned her attention to them, making sure they didn't burn. She had ten panforte to make for a wedding and she'd already scorched one batch of nuts. If she managed to destroy another she'd give up the shop, since she was clearly incapable of her chosen career. At least the candied peel was coming along as it should, bubbling happily in its syrupy bath.

She'd always found him attractive, even more now that he wasn't a floppy-haired adolescent. Could they make something together? He said he wanted to move back, which was good since she wasn't going anywhere. If he came back, if they made a relationship, it might even be easier once Bianca left.

But she couldn't leap into something that might be disastrous just because she feared being alone away from her twin. She had friends here, women she loved as much as her sister. She'd be fine.

She pulled the hazelnuts out of the oven just in time and dumped them into a bowl so they wouldn't scorch on the pan. She had no idea what was going on this evening, but she could wing it. She just had to trust that he could be more adult than she had been so many years ago.

One of the many blessings of short hair was that if it smelled like hazelnuts no one would notice unless they got far too close to her, so she could work up until it was time to go. All she had to do was change her t-shirt for a warmer top and her sneakers for heeled boots, both suitable for whatever might come next.

Bianca came home just as Josie was on her way out.

"Hey," Josie said, "you're not going anywhere tonight are you?"

"Nope. I'm gonna heat up the last of the lentil soup and try to finish that stupid game."

Relieved, Josie filled her in on her dinner with Simon and wished her a good night.

In the soft light of the restaurant Josie looked even more beautiful, Simon thought, then stashed that idea for later. He couldn't get distracted tonight or he'd lose his nerve and bail out of telling her his truth.

But still he wished this was a real date, the one they never got to have because he and Bianca had been awful, awful teenagers.

The server led them to a booth near the front window and left them alone with their menus. Simon stared at his for a bit, not really taking in the text, until Josie laughed. Startled, he looked up to see her putting down her menu. He lifted his eyebrows, questioning.

"This is ridiculous," she said, laughter still hiding in her smile. "We've known each other long enough; we shouldn't be nervous."

"Yet here we are."

"Exactly." She picked up her menu, glanced at it, then set it down again. "I'm having the beef cheeks. How 'bout you?"

Simon had to take a longer look at the small piece of paper in his hands. "The curry, I guess. Mom says hi."

"That's nice of her. How's she doing?"

"She's fine." It wasn't a lie, she was physically fine. "She volunteers at the library, now."

The conversation flowed easily from there, to the point where the server came to offer them dessert and they'd finished their meals without really noticing. They ordered tiny little crepes with lemon and icing sugar along with black tea and digestifs.

It was a cold walk from the restaurant back to Josie's place, but they were warm with food and liquor and good company, so neither of them really noticed. They took the back way, through the park along the river to see the lighted outdoor artwork. Other couples had had the same idea, and Simon watched them holding hands and suddenly yearned for even that much touch. So he grasped Josie's gloved hand in his bare one, smiling tentatively down at her when she looked over. She didn't frown or drop his hand, so he counted it as a win for tonight.

In the middle of the bridge she tugged on his hand, pulling him to a stop at the rail. Her smile was lovely, and for a moment he was sure she was going to kiss him here, under the lamplight in the gently falling snow. But instead she pulled something small out of her pocket, a caramel maybe, unwrapping it and tossing it into the river with a splash. She said something to the water.

"What was that?" he asked when she turned back to him.

Her cheeks flushed, and he reached out to touch the backs of his fingers to them, feeling their warmth for a second. "Oh. That was one of Taddeo's habits," she replied. "Drop a candy in the river and thank the forces we can't see."

He tried to keep the laugh out of his voice, he really did. "The forces are in the river?"

"Why wouldn't they be?"

He didn't have an answer to that. "Makes as much sense as any, I guess."

"As much sense as an old man in the sky, Grandpa always said."

And now she did kiss him, keeping him in place with a single hand on his chest, her chilled lips on his nearly stopping his heart. She backed away, her smile small and nervous.

"Okay?" she asked.

"Very okay," he replied. But as they grew closer to her home he argued with himself again, because he wasn't going to mess this up anymore, which meant he had to come clean.

They crossed the alley behind her building, still holding hands. Her smile sparkled in the light as she stopped at her door.

"You know," she said, taking a half step towards him. "I was a little worried this would be a prank."

"Nah, those days are over. Right?"

She settled in close to him before answering. "Right," she said softly.

Ignoring her hand on his chest and her face so close to his he focused over her shoulder, at the plain, dark wood door. "So I have to tell you something."

"Okay."

He gestured through the building behind her, in the direction of the Teufel building. "That's my job. I'm managing the restoration and opening of the Caldecutt store."

Her smile faded slightly. "I thought we said no pranks."

"I'm serious. That's why I'm in town." He rephrased. "That's why I'm home." He took a deep breath. "And full disclosure, I'm the one who suggested opening the first store here. In Concordia."

Her deliberately bland expression turned stony. She lifted her chin, dropped her hand, and said, "Good night, Simon." Then she turned her back and unlocked the door.

"Good night."

She didn't turn back as she closed the door, and the solid thunk as the deadbolt slid home echoed through his heart.

Josie resolutely climbed the stairs after she locked the door behind her. She wouldn't think about him anymore. He had told her the truth before they got too involved and that was commendable, but they were done for good now.

She bypassed her own apartment and headed up to Bianca's, stopping only to shut off her phone. She knocked softly in case Bianca was sleeping, but the door opened almost immediately.

Her sister looked at her and her bright face fell as she noticed Josie's mood. "Oh," she said. "That bad? I've got tea."

Bianca's living room didn't hold the weight of generations that Josie's did; it had only been their childhood playroom, and so got redone several times as they grew up. The whole floor had been renovated for them to share during university, and it had reflected the chaos of their lives at the time. Now it was a pleasant box of quiet blues and greens, as soft and feminine as Bianca herself.

Josie took her boots and coat off and stowed them in the closet before collapsing on the velvet love seat under the window. Snow fell gently, sparingly, past the powerful street lamp out front. It was early this year, but not terribly so; her parents had often shared stories of having to trick or treat in snow suits back in the '70s, and she had vague memories of a Thanksgiving parade with snow, the dry, icy kind instead of this pretty fluff.

Bianca came back with tea, handing Josie her favourite mug, the one with the chicken on it. Bergamot wafted up with the steam and Josie just smelled it for a while before drinking.

"So what happened?"

Josie told her everything, every detail of the evening, just so Bianca could feel the same betrayal she had at the end of the story.

Bianca's expression changed from calm listening Bianca to angry Bianca to sympathetic Bianca all in a flash. "That seems," she paused, "unlike him."

"That's what I would have thought, but he said it, flat out. He's responsible for Caldecutt coming in to destroy my business."

Bianca hummed, then stared out the window at the snow for a moment. "Do you mind if I talk to him?"

Josie shrugged, done with this conversation. "Go ahead. In fact, let him know that he's not allowed in my store anymore." It was petty and probably ineffective, but she was feeling petty and ineffective right now. "I need to stop thinking. Want to play some Fortnite?"

Without even answering, Bianca got out her Xbox controllers and turned on the TV.

The next morning, Josie worked at putting last night out of her mind; she never wanted to dwell on failure, instead working to make herself better. But this wasn't her failure, wasn't something she could improve, so all she could do was try to calm the sting of betrayal. Last night, putting all her emotions into killing opponents and collecting equipment had helped immensely, but the baking she had to do now was second nature, leaving her plenty of time to think. She rushed through the usual selection and then after the morning rush worked on a couple of new-to-her recipes, things that would occupy her attention. That she'd have to perfect.

It helped that she loved Halloween – the churchy holidays were fine, but Halloween really got her creativity moving. So as the last batch of blood cookies baked she got out the decorations she'd been working on all year. Many were reworked versions of her old ones, but she liked to have a kind of theme each year for the trick or treaters. This year she was going to be a swamp witch, which meant her decorations were mostly green and black and brown, with lots of glistening eyeballs and wet-looking tentacles peering out from ragged foliage. She cackled to herself as she redecorated the display case, tearing down the paper pumpkins and fall leaves and replacing them with plastic insects and dyed reindeer moss. She put a small apothecary case that Bianca had made on the counter and added little bottles of coloured goo to each nook, then thought better of it and used museum wax to attach each bottle to its shelf. The last thing to go up, in honour of her grandfather, was the creepy carved wood thing – he never told her exactly what it was but it looked like tangled-up snaky things made of fire or smoke or something, but alive. He put it up every year right beside his river monster.

After a couple of hours' work she realized that she hadn't thought about Simon at all; it wasn't until she saw someone coming out of the worksite gate that she remembered. She recognized Dave as he crossed the street, and decided that if he came in she'd ask him out. But he didn't, he merely waved at her through the window with a smile before moving on.

At five she closed up the shop and grabbed whatever wrapped candy was closest to take to the bridge. She needed a little luck.

Simon spent the morning trying to find a way out. He went over the building plans again and again, hoping to spot a flaw that would, if reported, make Caldecutt withdraw and sell the building off. But he had done his job too well the past few years and he could find nothing. He scoured local records, hoping that Teufel had been a Nazi or that the building had been home to a notorious murder, but public record showed nothing except a string of failed businesses and a couple of oddly-timed near-disasters. How did you manage to have a building catch fire twice fifty years apart to the day?

He even went back to the purchase records but found nothing he could covertly send to Josie's lawyer. By that point he was feeling guilty for getting paid to undermine his employer so he gave up and took a walking tour of the work site. Two months in, the abatement was finished and the new drywall was up. Refinishing the Douglas fir floors was next on the agenda; he'd fought hard to keep those floors instead of discarding them in favour of tile and he was excited to see them as they were meant to be. He couldn't save the plaster mouldings or the tin ceiling in situ, but he had chunks of them in his office to put on display as a nod to the building's original grandeur. At least the building owners were doing a better job at saving the upper floors for other future tenants. But Caldecutt was rich and loud so what they wanted was what was done.

Simon greeted the workers on his way past as they taped the seams in the walls, noting with a stab of guilt the box from Josie's on a table near the door. The reason he'd fought to save the floors and ceiling and plaster was to curry goodwill with a city whose history was so recent that they'd barely had time to respect it. He'd wanted to make a mark, to be the company that understood craftsmanship, and now he realized that he was naive. You couldn't just become that company, you had to build it from the ground up the way Josie's grandfather had.

Keeping the floors had gone a long way toward boosting Caldecutt's reputation, but the plastering company that did the cornices was still in business three generations later and so the local paper had also done an article on them and the hours of work that it took to create such fragile beauty.

Something simmered in the back of Simon's mind but he couldn't quite catch it yet. Had it been a bylaw? Something in the rental agreement? Historical preservation didn't have to be just about buildings; perhaps it could be about a way of life as well, something this city did know about considering the large Mennonite population in the surrounding area. If the giant chain supermarket had to put stables in their parking lots, then perhaps there was a legacy bylaw he could make fit this situation.

The renovations wouldn't be finished until spring, so he had plenty of time to figure something out.

His office on the second floor didn't have drywall yet, as the construction orders specified finishing the retail space first. He had a small desk facing the window, a good chair, and a light, but that was about it. When the store opened the manager's office would be on the ground floor, but that wouldn't happen until the painters came in.

It was getting cold up here in the barely insulated space, so he gathered his work to take it over to Josie's. It wasn't until he was nearly at the door that he remembered she didn't want him there, that she had specifically ordered him away. He prepared to go to the café down the street when he heard Bianca calling his name.

He looked up at the balcony and saw her waving down at him.

"Come around the back," she said, pointing through her apartment. "I'll let you in."

Confused but willing to play along, he cut through the alley to the back, where Bianca waited with the heavy door open. "What's up?" he asked, following her inside.

"I wanted to talk to you. Let's go up to my place."

He followed her up the stairs. "Won't Josie be mad at you?"

Bianca looked back at him. "She can't order me around. Well she can," she said, starting up the stairs again, "but I don't have to listen."

They got to her landing and she opened the door, inviting him in. "And anyway, she said I could talk to you. She's not entirely unreasonable," she added.

Simon had nothing to say to that. Josie was not at fault here. He shucked his jacket but left his shoes on, since Bianca hadn't invited him past the doormat. She stood in front of him, arms crossed, face like stone.

"Why?" she asked. "Why would you do this?"

He bristled. "I thought this would be good for the city. When I--"

"Good?" she interrupted. "How could this be good for anything but your pay raise?"

He raised his hand as if to ward her off, then thought better of it and brought it back down to his pocket. "As I was about to say, when I left, this downtown was a hole. I didn't know the shop was still open! I hadn't been back in years!"

"You couldn't use Google Maps? You couldn't check our website?" Her voice rose with every question and Simon wondered if Josie could hear. "You couldn't call? You just ignored this side of the street?"

She was putting him in a defensive position, which he hated, and it unfortunately showed in his tone. "The location wasn't my choice. And when I found out it was River I didn't look up the cross street. The chances were low that it was in downtown."

"Oh, right. Because nothing changes over a decade, eh?'

He slumped against the door, giving up. "Mom always acted like it hadn't."

That surprised her. "She never comes downtown?"

"She doesn't have to."

Bianca turned away suddenly, taking a few steps farther into her apartment. "The growth because of the tech sector moving in has been in all the news!"

"She only cares about the paper for the crossword."

"And you had more important things to care about," she snapped as she whirled back to him.

"Yes. And I'm not happy about that. I was an ass and this job just made me into more of one. I am deeply sorry."

Bianca deflated, her muscles losing their previous tension. "You need to say that to her.

"Josie poured everything she had into this shop. Every moment of her education past high school was about taking over from Dad and making Grandpa proud of her. She had a year of perfection, after Mom and Dad moved to Italy and before Grandpa died. If this store, your store, drives her out of business what will she do? She'll have to sell the building, probably, to start new somewhere else. You're putting her out of her business and her home. I hope you realize that."

Simon had nothing to say, and she added, over his silence, "Everything that made us who we are happened in this building." And to his mortification her eyes welled with tears.

"Bianca."

She wiped her eyes with the back of her hand. "I don't even know why I'm crying right now."

"I'm sorry. I'm saying it to you right now. I'm so very sorry."

She nodded, not really looking at him.

"But I think I have a way to fix some of the damage."

Bianca's head shot up, eyes fixed on him. "Tell me."

"Josie, you're being unreasonable."

Josie ignored her sister, instead watching the mixer full of marshmallow, waiting for it to be perfect.

Bianca tried again, this time closing the oven door a little too hard to get Josie's attention. "You can't keep up like this."

She had Josie's attention—everything in this kitchen had Josie's attention because it was Josie's life—but Josie wouldn't let on. She stopped the mixer, knowing without having to check that the marshmallow would form beautiful drapey peaks when she took the whisk out. One of her favourite things about baking was that a lot of it was just instinct and paying attention. A practiced baker or candymaker could smell when the cookies were ready to come out of the oven, or know just by timing when the sugar syrup had reached hard crack stage.

Smoothing the marshmallow out into the pan to set, Josie continued to ignore Bianca while carefully listening to everything she said. Yes, she was being unreasonable. Yes, she had taken on too much work. No, she didn't need to slow down, because if she did she'd think once again about how empty her life was aside from the shop and Bianca.

She cut off that train of thought almost as it began. "Turn on some music, please Bianca?" She pulled the sugar cookie dough out of the fridge and transferred it to the big stainless steel bench with a thump.

Mom's Punk Playlist started up with a crash of guitar and Josie slipped on a fresh pair of gloves and rolled the dough to an eyeballed quarter inch for Bianca to cut out. The music kept her moving, kept her from thinking as she screeched the lyrics out in her head along with the lead singer.

When that was done she moved on to making non-Halloween-themed candy, the usual nougat and fruit jellies (although some of those were Halloweeny too – her witch flavour was very popular), truffles and caramels. Make one, set it to cool, start on another, Bianca following behind her at regular intervals to slice or wrap or shape. This was the work of a Sunday morning; her grandfather called it his church and she and Bianca had kept up the habit. Truffle and hard candy flavours changed frequently, to keep Josie and her customers from getting bored. Some of her regulars came in only to try what was new and interesting, others stuck with their favourites. She also kept a small selection of imported candy and cookies for sale, which regularly filled out gift baskets and party favours. She could do this. She could survive.

As she moved from kitchen to store she noticed a new flyer on the public corkboard. As always she checked it out, making sure it was nothing hateful. What she found was an announcement, a call for people to attend a protest outside Caldecutt's store, organized by "Concordia Friends of Small Business". She took a picture and texted it to Ekua. "Are you behind this?" she asked.

She got a reply a few minutes later, a simple, "No, but we'll attend if we can. Teach them all a lesson about unity."

Josie tucked her phone in her apron and went over to stare at the paper again as if that would release its secrets to her. The protest was Wednesday starting at eight and running 'til dusk. She wished them well.

At eight on Wednesday morning picketers began to show up, soon followed by news crews. She recognized a few people, but most were strangers to her. At noon she took a couple dozen jellies out and passed them around with her thanks, which caught the attention of the reporters, which led to her making a little speech thanking everyone for coming and no, she hadn't organized this but she was flattered that someone had. A news crew from Toronto came into the store later to interview her and clarify matters for viewers outside Concordia.

"Everyone loves a little guy story," one reporter said off-hand, to which Josie replied, "And yet they shop at the big guy's store. I promise you, just one of my chocolates is more satisfying than a whole bar of theirs."

When asked to explain, she continued, "This is just my experience, but I find that simpler recipes make for better chocolates. All the fillers in cheap chocolate mean you have to eat more to be satisfied, but a good, simple chocolate recipe will make you happy with less of it. Now cheap chocolate has it's place, definitely. I know that the average birthday party of twenty kids needs cheaper chocolate, but if we're talking about an occasional treat? I'll go for purity over price anytime."

Was invoking purity manipulative? Probably. But she'd had these talking points ready to go for a while now and was happy to use them no matter the occasion. And she did speak the truth of her experience; she did find she needed to eat more of a cheap chocolate to feel satisfied. Caldecutt was slightly above cheap chocolate, but why mention that?

Josie had assumed that when the protesters left at dusk that that would be it – just a little light disturbance in an otherwise usual day. But they were there the next day, too, and the one after that, until they became a part of the scenery to Josie and she almost forgot why they were there.

And as customers trickled in to pick up their Halloween orders that week they mentioned the protest, or the interview, or their own shifts making signs or standing on the sidewalk and informing drivers of why they were there. Several articles popped up in the local papers, as well as opinion pieces, and Josie grew suspicious. There was no way her little store had made that much of an impact. The city was so big you didn't ever have to pass her store if you didn't want to. Someone had to be organizing this, and it wasn't the Downtown Business Association.

It had to be Bianca.

But when questioned, even when treated to Josie's homemade hot chocolate, Bianca stood firm. She wasn't behind it. Josie did get the feeling Bianca knew who was, and perhaps had even helped them, but she couldn't pry that information out of her twin.

7

Simon spent October 31st mired in paperwork, entangled in phone calls. His bosses didn't like the amount of media attention the protest was getting; they feared that the longer it went on the more of a story it would become, eliminating their impact when they opened. Simon was glad his bosses weren't there to see him smile at their worry. There was no way this store wouldn't make a profit and lead to more stores elsewhere in the country, but capitalism liked to scream and dance around like a cartoon elephant confronted by a mouse at the slightest hint of dissent.

He had actively been ordered to remove the picketers, but he managed to convince his direct report that doing anything more than politely asking them to leave would be even worse for their reputation. So he ended up going downstairs, out the back, and around the building to politely ask them to leave. Then he waited while they laughed at him, listened to one of the older protesters berate him for betraying his father, "who always shopped local. He was the reason my hardware store lasted as long as it did. And don't you laugh, Patty, I know what you're thinking."

Several phone cameras were pointed at him, so Simon wished everyone a good afternoon and went back upstairs to report on his delightful failure.

But the afternoon wasn't turning out so good. The early morning forecast had called for high winds and some snow later on, with dire warnings for trick-or-treaters. But the snow was already falling at three and by the time he left work the sky was completely dark. He quickly texted his sister to make sure Mom got there okay.

Standing outside, watching big fat flakes come down faster than looked possible, the sky dark and the thick snow reflecting all the street and shops lights, Simon could almost believe he was alone. There were trick-or-treaters all over, rushing to get their bags filled before their parents made them go home, cars heading out to the suburbs, all the usual evening sounds of a city, but the snow insulated him from it all. He loved nights like this. He stood there a few more minutes, waving to the protesters as they left, until a particularly icy gust of wind drove him up the street for dinner.

He was just finishing his meal when the power went out.

"Sorry, sorry," the server said as he came into the dining room with a flashlight and a couple of LED candles. He set a candle in front of Simon, then the few other diners, then announced to the room, "The whole block is out, along with a few other parts of the city. Trees are coming down all over the place. We're going to have to ask you to finish up quickly so we can get this place cleaned and get home before the roads get too slick."

Another customer called the server over and Simon checked how much cash he had. He was lucky, he had enough to cover his dal makhani and tea as well as leave a tip. When the server was free again Simon paid, picked up his coat, hat, and gloves and ventured out the front door.

A wall of ice pellets slammed into him, all the beautiful fat flakes gone in place of what would be hail if it was summer, and all of it was coming sideways from the direction he had to walk. There was no point in trying to get a bus, the nearest stop was about halfway between here and his hotel anyway. He checked up the street to see if the hotel had power, but he couldn't see anything. Not that he just couldn't see lights, but he couldn't see a damn thing in the sky above about ten feet, not even the buildings nearest him. The snow on the sidewalk was already over his ankles and rising steadily.

This wasn't just a pain in the ass, this was life-threatening. But all he could do was stumble in the right direction and hope. He wrapped his scarf over his hat and around his neck, making a frame around his face to keep him a little warmer. He looked like a babushka but there wasn't anyone around to care anyway.

Josie shivered as a wave of pelleted snow hit the window with a crackle, suddenly glad she lived in the same building she worked in. The trick-or-treaters had all scattered as the weather worsened, and she'd tidied the store before the power went out, so now she was splitting all the perishable leftover Halloween goodies into two boxes by the light of her emergency lantern. She'd give one to Bianca and keep one for herself; she didn't always abstain from eating her own goods.

Her phone rang and Bianca's name flashed on the screen, so she scrambled to answer.

"Hey, what's up?"

"Is there power over there?"

"Nope. Went out about half an hour ago."

"Right. I'm staying here for the night, then."

"Where?"

"At Vichai's."

"Okay. I'm battening down the hatches right now."

"Hey, one other thing. I got a call from Simon."

Josie bristled a bit. This was not the time. Except it turned out it was.

"He's huddled in the doorway a few stores down," Bianca continued. "Will you let him in?"

What the actual fuck. "Of course I will. I'll call him myself."

Bianca said goodbye quickly and Josie dialled Simon immediately. "Hey, get over here," she said when he answered. "Come to the shop door."

"Thanks," he said, shivering evident in his voice.

As she poured the last cup of lukewarm tea for him, she heard thumping on the door. Unable to see anything outside, she doused the light and was just able to make out the shadow of a man. Simon.

She opened the door only as far as necessary to let him in, then closed and locked it tightly behind him. He was trembling, barely even able to get an apology out before she started stripping him of his freezing outer clothes.

"Did you really think I'd let you die outside my own building? Or at all?" she ranted, kneeling to untie his thankfully appropriate winter boots.

His teeth chattered in response. "No. Not really. It's just, Bianca's number was at the top of my contacts list."

That was fair. She pulled his boots off and set them on the rubber mat. "Okay. And just so you know, I wouldn't turn down shelter to anyone who's about to freeze, enemy or otherwise."

She pulled a towel from her apron and wiped the icy water from his face, then reached over to the counter to grab the tea. "Here, drink this. It's not hot, but it's probably warmer than you are."

He gulped it down, lips so cold he could barely form a seal on the cup, and she tried to act casual as she wiped the tea from his chin.

He laughed, wet and broken. "Sorry."

"No problem." His now-sopping outerwear taken care of, she gestured out the back towards the kitchen. "I'm done here, so let's go upstairs. I'll build a fire."

He nodded and started walking, still clutching the cup. Josie flipped the light switches so they wouldn't all be on when the power came back, then locked up the kitchen and followed him upstairs.

Her apartment was warmer than the store and Simon stopped to bask in it for a minute. "You mind if I take off my socks? They're still a bit wet."

"Sure, go ahead," she replied, heading for the kitchen to put the kettle on, lighting the gas stove with a match. When that was done she built the fire, the first one this winter, allowing that to keep her from getting angry again. It was lucky she already had the kindling split; she almost hadn't done it the other day but she wanted to take out her anger on something and blocks of wood and an axe were decent enough substitutes.

"You want a fresh pair of socks? Or some sweats? I might have some that fit you."

"Whatever you want to give me, I'll take."

Josie swung by the kitchen to make the tea and then found her largest pair of flannel pants and her giant wool socks, dropping them off to him before retreating to the kitchen again. She heard the bathroom door close, then open again a couple of minutes later, and she couldn't avoid him any longer because the cinnamon tea was done steeping.

He was on the couch wrapped in the blanket her grandma crocheted, leaning close to the heat from the fire. "After I've finished my tea I'll be warm enough to go out there again."

"You're staying the night," she said, punctuating it with the thump of his mug on the coffee table.

"I'm clearly making you uncomfortable."

"You'd make me even more uncomfortable if they found you in the morning frozen to the steps of your hotel." She sat beside him and picked up her laptop, setting it on the table in front of them.

"I watch horror movies on Halloween, so that's what we're doing. I had actually planned to listen to a horror podcast," she said, flipping through the catalogue looking for a modern gothic adaptation she'd been saving. "But it's better to save my phone battery."

"So what's your policy on talking during movies?" Simon asked. He pulled his feet up on the couch between them and settled even deeper into the blanket.

"Film-related only."

Ten minutes into the movie found them silent except for incidental sounds – Simon taking off the blanket now that he was warm again, Josie finishing her tea and setting the cup down, the crackle of the fire and the sleet against the window. There would be a thick layer of ice tomorrow, you could already see it forming on the glass, warping what little view there was.

As always, Josie fervently hoped the old panes wouldn't break, a thought that got her up and banking the fire. The room was warm enough already, and she closed the heavy drapes to help it stay that way. She loved this old building, it was part of the family, but like any ageing family member it could be cranky and annoying at times.

When she sat back down she claimed the middle cushion, leaning against Simon's sturdy shoulder with a sigh.

"Does this mean you forgive me?"

She had to think about that. "I don't know," she ended up with. "This just feels right. I've missed you."

"You were one person in my life I could always rely on," he said quietly.

"I didn't know that."

"I always knew how you'd react. Except that one time."

Josie shifted, turning a little to see him. "Which time?"

"The date I took Bianca on." Simon turned to face her, too, laying his head on the back of the chesterfield. "I knew you'd be pissed. I didn't know you'd be hurt."

"That might have been the moment I realized you weren't just playing with me. I guess I," she hesitated. "I felt like I'd missed something important. I wasn't used to not being sure of what was going on."

"And that was my daily life, except for you."

Josie almost said something snide, like a comment about how fucked up that was, but she didn't want to change the mood. "Still, you knowingly went out with my twin instead of me."

"You forgave her, didn't you? And anyway, you got me back when you fucked my sister."

"Does she still blush when you mention me?"

"No," he said, looking petulant. Somehow she didn't believe him.

"She does stutter a little, though. And my best friend!" he added, still looking at the forgotten movie.

Josie gave him a dreamy smile.

"At the same time!"

Her smile widened into a grin. "That was a great party." She poked him in the thigh to get his full attention. "You know, I'd have fucked you instead if you hadn't been a snob all year."

He froze for a second, thoughts written all over his face. "I was terrible, wasn't I."

"Yep. Your crowning moment, I believe, was coming back here and telling all of us how we'd never get out of our hick town and make something of ourselves if we didn't do it now." It still hurt a bit to think about. "As if it was impossible to make something of yourself in the place you grew up. As if 'making something of yourself' was the only real way to live."

"I'm sorry. I think I knew at the time that it was complete bullshit, but…. Actually I have no excuse. I was full of myself."

She patted his knee. "At least you grew out of it."

He huffed. "As if you weren't just as bad when you came back from France or wherever."

"Yeah, well, at least I learned a trade," she replied with a grin, "and not whatever it is you do. What is it you do anyway?"

He closed his eyes as if pained. "I'm not even sure these days. I mostly answer questions from contractors and deliver orders from my manager."

"Are you not happy with your job?"

"Haven't been for a while."

"And?"

"And I've been looking for a new job here for a couple of weeks now."

"Okay."

"Can I explain? I feel like I should explain."

It was Josie's turn to stare at the movie, not really seeing the images flashing by. "Sure," she finally said.

"I never intended to hurt you. I hope you know that."

In her moments of quiet thought she had come to realize that, yes. Their tricks had never had permanent consequences; even as they met again last month they'd come together as friends, not enemies.

"I do."

He took a deep breath, letting it out with, "Mom's cognition has been sliding, these past few years."

Startled, Josie turned to him. "But she's so young!"

He told her everything – about the lapses, the confusion, the small moments that meant nothing on their own but added up to something very bad. Simon shook his head, running a hand through his hair as he did. "I don't know what's going on because she won't admit it's a problem. She won't see a doctor and I'm going to make sure she does."

"I wish I could help," she said finally.

"It's just nice to have someone to tell who isn't Alyssa. She worries enough." He slumped, sinking down into the couch cushions. "All I wanted to do was have a reason to come home for a while and look after her."

"I can understand that," Josie replied, her voice cracking a bit.

"Right now I can't figure out why I thought taking this job was a good idea, but I was a little desperate. I can't quit outright and hope to find a job here in good time. And I don't want to get stuck living with Mom for the rest of her life."

He was rambling now, anguish pouring off him with every word, every movement, and he didn't care enough to stop it. Overwhelmed, Josie tucked herself into his chest, holding him together while he kept talking.

He squeezed her tight before he spoke again. "She might think she wants that, but she doesn't."

Then Simon told her every word he'd told Bianca, about how he hadn't known the shop was still around, how he'd never thought to check the exact location. How he would have fought it if he'd known. How sorry he was.

Something he said must have clicked for Josie; she'd always been smarter than people thought. She sat up straight, her hands landing on his chest to push herself away. "You're the one behind the protests."

He nodded. "It was my idea. Bianca did the organizing."

She hugged him hard, this time, holding him in gratitude rather than comfort. He sighed into her hair, and she let him pull her right into his lap.

"Are they having any effect?" she asked, her breath heating his neck.

"I don't know. A little, maybe. They don't like that it's going on but they won't take any action yet."

Josie slid away with a sigh, staying in his lap but pulling back far enough to look at him. "We can only hope."

He chuckled. "Yeah. There's tons of time; we won't be ready to install counters and everything until spring."

"I'll just have to wow everyone at Christmas, then."

"I think you wowed everyone today, honestly."

"Thanks," she said. "And thanks for not letting me get away with anger."

"I'm sure you would have come to your senses eventually," he replied, grinning.

She scoffed at him, then slid away and closed the now-quiet laptop. "I need to get to bed." She paused for a second, cups in one hand, flashlight in the other. "Are you going to be okay out here?"

"Yeah."

"There's extra toothbrushes and stuff in the bottom left bathroom drawer."

"Okay."

She took a few steps away, then stopped again. "I'll bring you some pillows and blankets in a minute." Then all he could see was her flashlight disappearing into the kitchen.

Simon got up and peered out the window again, but all he could see was dull grey movement and icy glass. He dropped the curtain and lit up his own phone's flashlight to examine the bookcase, just for something to do. As he expected it was full of cookbooks, textbooks, and the gothic mysteries and horror she'd always loved. He suspected the e-reader tucked in with them was full of similar genres.

A whole shelf of books had Italian titles and must have belonged to her grandparents, given the age of them. He wondered if she read them at all, and if so, what she'd learned about them as people. He'd barely known his grandparents, most of them having passed when he was small. Was that why he felt so lost most of the time and she was so certain of her place in the world? He brushed that thought aside, knowing it would keep him awake all night if he dwelled on it.

Josie came back with an armful of mismatched bedding and began laying it out for him. "I'm really sorry I don't have a bed in the guest room, but it broke last winter and I haven't replaced it yet."

Simon helped her spread out the sheets and blankets. "It's all right. This couch seems comfortable enough."

"It really is. I nap on it pretty often." She plopped the pillow down at one end and smoothed the wrinkles out of the case. "Still, if you can't sleep for any reason, just knock on my door. It'll wake me up."

He just said, "Okay," again, feeling like in his fatigue he'd regressed to bare politeness. "Thanks."

"No problem."

Then she was gone again, this time down the hallway to her bedroom.

He woke confused and too warm with light seeping around the edges of the curtains and a buzz of formless noise outside. He checked the time, but it was far too early for the sun to be that bright, or even out at all.

Getting up, Simon pulled the curtain aside a bit, just to see what was going on, only to wake up completely when he noticed the smoke seeping out of the lower windows of the Teufel building. His building.

Now the noise from below made sense – firefighters and police, onlookers and news crews, all crowding in front of Josie's store. Shit. He needed to wake her up. He needed to call his boss.

He stared at his phone for a second, trying to figure out what to do first, but his feet were already taking him down the hall, past the bathroom—the power must have come on while he was asleep, since a nightlight was on—to her bedroom door. He knocked gently, then realized that was pointless and knocked purposefully to wake her up.

"Who?" he heard from inside, then, "Oh. Simon?"

"Can I come in?"

"Sure."

Her room was completely dark, not even the light from a clock, and silent, being at the back of the building. Sheets rustled as she sat up, and a soft glow emanated from behind her headboard. "What's up?" she said with a yawn.

"There's a fire across the street."

Horror flashed over her face until she registered 'across the street,' then she rolled out of bed and into her slippers, brushing past him out the door. He caught up to her just as she opened the floor length living room curtains wide.

"Wow," she said, wiping some condensation off the glass. "That place really is cursed."

"Thank god the neighbouring buildings are just offices." They were, in fact, a bank and a branch of an international accounting firm, so no real loss there. And he knew Caldecutt had the whole operation insured. They'd probably make a small profit off the deal.

"Yeah. What do you think happened?"

They both flinched as part of the facade crashed down to the sidewalk, missing a pair of firefighters below. Oddly, the still saw no flames, just an odd light, intense heat, and a lot of smoke.

"I just hope it's not arson," Josie said, wrapping her arms around herself with a shiver. "We're ramping up to Christmas. I don't have time to be under investigation right now."

"You've got a great alibi." Simon sighed, realizing he should really call his manager's office and leave a message. "Nobody will suspect I was in on it."

Josie laughed a little, which was his only goal at the moment. "Until they dig up that you were behind the protests."

"Bianca will take the fall for me."

"I'm sure. I should see if she's awake." Josie dug around in the pocket of her flannel pants and pulled out her phone.

Simon took the opportunity to leave his manager a message, then pulled a chair around to watch out the window. The heat coming off the fire was so intense it was melting all the snow on Josie's window.

"I'm probably going to have to repaint the frame," Josie said, leaning against him. "Come with me downstairs to check the shop?"

He stood and slipped her thick socks back on before joining her in the hall, where she was talking to someone upstairs. Her tenants, he guessed, since Bianca wasn't home. The others stepped back inside their apartment and Josie came back down the few stairs to lead him to the shop.

She flicked a single light on in the back, guessing correctly that the front would be well-lit from the rescue vehicles. Near the windows it was warm, but not hot enough to affect her paint, so that was good. He stood beside her, wrapping one arm around her when she shivered again.

"There but for the grace of blah blah blah," she said, clearly joking but also gravely serious.

Simon tried to look at him from her point of view. If this was merely a glitch from faulty wiring when the power came back on it might well have been her building, her store, her people, and though insurance would cover it she'd be losing more than just money, more than just a business. In that moment his heart ached for that other Josie, that other Bianca.

"Hey," Josie said quietly. As he turned to her she raised herself up on her tiptoes, drifting closer to him than ever before. "Life is short."

Then she kissed him.

As her lips touched his, soft and warm and wet, Josie's heart pounded in her ears until he softened, melding his lips and body to her in wholehearted acceptance. His tongue peeked out to touch hers and she shivered; he had a delicate touch, and she should not be so aroused by something so simple, but she couldn't help but lean in to him, pressing close, sipping from his mouth like ambrosia.

A noise outside pulled them away from each other only enough to watch as the ground under the Teufel building seemed to ripple, sending the rescue workers running outwards in all directions to find safe ground.

Josie watched, perplexed for a moment. "Was that an earthquake?"

Simon slowly shook his head. "I don't think so."

The view opened up for them as the ground continued to move and shift, rippling out in their direction. The sidewalk cracked and the asphalt seemed to melt before reforming into almost sand-like grains.

"Quicksand?" Simon asked.

"We are built on an aquifer," Josie replied, compelled to stare at the base of the building.

The back door of their building slammed shut behind them as the tenants presumably evacuated. "We should leave," Josie said, but couldn't make herself move.

"Yeah." Simon breathed the word, sounding as awestruck as Josie felt.

The ripples stopped short of the yellow line diving the street, bouncing back as if they'd hit a seawall. Josie and Simon watched as they rolled back towards the building. The moment they hit the far sidewalk again the building shuddered, and a giant thing, like an appendage that was far too big and smooth while still having inexplicable texture, rose out of the foundation and wrapped itself around the whole building in a spiral of visual uncertainty.

Cold washed over Josie despite the lingering heat and she wondered if she was having a cerebral event.

"Do you see that?" Simon asked, his hands tightening on Josie's waist.

"Yes." She didn't relax, and her relief was out of proportion to the situation when he proved she wasn't alone in her delusion.

"What is it?"

Her voice creaked as she replied, "I have no idea."

Almost as quickly as it rose, the tentacle crushed the building in its grip, pulling it and the fire back down into the concrete sludge. And then there was nothing.

Nothing else on the street was disturbed. Although Josie knew she could still hear the hum of the freezers in the kitchen, a pervasive quiet was also present.

Outside the bystanders were silent, some moving slowly towards the now-empty building site, some still staring at the same spot.

Reporters checked their cameras, playing back the video and then shaking their heads in confusion.

Other than that, everything was normal.

Josie's brain came back online after a moment. "I guess they can't blame that on me."

Simon chuckled, his eyes still wide in wonder. "I didn't," he stopped, then started again. "How?" was what he settled on.

A stray memory hit Josie hard, of standing on the bridge with her grandfather and tossing a single hard candy into the river. "To thank those we cannot see," he'd told her. She said it aloud to Simon, then repeated, "those we cannot see. I always thought he meant luck or dead family, but maybe," she gestured wildly toward the opposite side of the street. "Maybe he meant that."

Simon took a step towards the window. "Thank you," he said forcefully. "Thank you for solving our problem for us."

Struck by the sheer impossibility of the situation, Josie began to laugh, and if she was a little hysterical about it at least no one but Simon could see.

"The building really was cursed," she stammered out between startled laughs.

Simon grinned at her. "I guess the elder gods hate monopolies, too."

Laughed out, Josie twined her arm with his and tugged him with her to the back. "Come on. I desperately need to sleep so I can forget this happened."

He followed her upstairs, and when she led him to her bedroom he didn't resist.

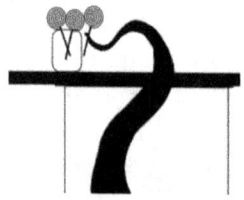